"*The operative word is 'sleeping.'*

You and I know that," Lark said huskily, "but I'm afraid your daughter would never have believed it."

"Smart girl, my daughter," he said, and touched his lips to hers. "I can hardly believe it myself. My age must be catching up with me."

"Not age," she whispered, "time zones." Her eyes widened. "That is, unless you found the company unexciting."

Jonathan groaned softly. "Believe me, the company was exciting, but thank God I was too exhausted to do anything about it. If I hadn't been, I wouldn't have stayed, and last night I needed you in my arms. I reached for you when I woke up," he added, "and I felt abandoned when you weren't there beside me."

"You may have forgotten, but you have a small daughter who wakens early. This morning it was six o'clock. I got out of bed quickly and went to her so she wouldn't wake you up, too."

"Oh, Lark," he said in a tone that sounded like a cross between amusement and regret. "I'm afraid your virtue is safe around here. H̲a̲v̲e̲ ̲t̲o̲ ̲r̲e̲p̲l̲a̲ce you with a hous̲e̲ every move? I g̲ living like a mo̲

Dear Reader,

Welcome to Silhouette. Experience the magic of the wonderful world where two people fall in love. Meet heroines who will make you cheer for their happiness, and heroes (be they the boy next door or a handsome, mysterious stranger) who will win your heart. Silhouette Romances reflect the magic of love—sweeping you away with books that make will you laugh and cry, heartwarming, poignant stories that will move you time and time again.

In the next few months, we're publishing romances by many of your all-time favorites, such as Diana Palmer, Brittany Young, Emilie Richards and Arlene James. Your response to these authors and other authors of Silhouette Romances has served as a touchstone for us, and we're pleased to bring you more books with Silhouette's distinctive medley of charm, wit and—above all—*romance*.

I hope you enjoy this book and the many stories to come. Experience the magic!

Sincerely,

Tara Hughes
Senior Editor
Silhouette Books

PHYLLIS HALLDORSON
An Honest Lover

Silhouette *Romance*

Published by Silhouette Books New York

America's Publisher of Contemporary Romance

For the third generation: Lisa, Heather,
Michael, Greg, Glenn, Teddy, Marina, Megan,
Billy and Sarah.
Our joy in the present, our hope for the future.

SILHOUETTE BOOKS
300 E. 42nd St., New York, N.Y. 10017

ISBN: 0-373-08456-0

First Silhouette Books printing September 1986

America's Publisher of Contemporary Romance

Printed in the U.S.A.

Books by Phyllis Halldorson

Silhouette Romance

Temporary Bride #31
To Start Again #79
Mountain Melody #247
If Ever I Loved You #282
Design for Two Hearts #367
Forgotten Love #395
An Honest Lover #456

Silhouette Special Edition

My Heart's Undoing #290

PHYLLIS HALLDORSON,

like all her heroines, is as in love with her husband today as on the day they met. It is because she has known so much love in her own life that her characters seem to come alive as they, too, discover the joys of romance.

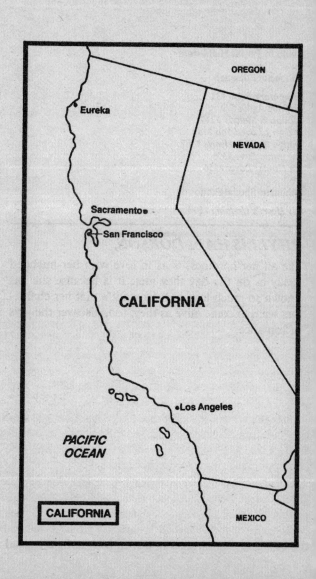

Chapter One

Lark slowed her elderly blue Mustang to a crawl in an effort to read the identifying numbers on the buildings. She'd only arrived in Eureka the day before, and in spite of her brother Rob's detailed instructions for finding his office she'd managed to get lost. You'd think anyone who'd lived all her twenty-five years in Phoenix wouldn't have much trouble finding her way around a city as small as this one on the northern coast of California, but then, Lark had an impaired sense of direction that had plagued her all her life.

She spotted a large *554* painted on a signboard in front of one building. Logically, number 558 should be two doors farther up. She drew a sigh of relief and pulled into an empty parking space along the curb.

Rob had mentioned that his office was on the second floor, but he hadn't told her it was in such a new and imposing building. In fact, over the five years he'd been in business here, she'd had the impression from his letters that the building was rather run-down. Maybe he'd moved recently, but if so he hadn't mentioned it. Of course, last night she'd been so excited about seeing Rob and Melanie and their two small sons, and catching up on all those years apart, that it wouldn't be surprising if they'd missed a few things.

The elevator stopped on the second floor, and she followed the discreet signs to room 205. The name on the door was Bishop, Caldwell and Bergen. Lark blinked. It should have read Carlisle Private Investigations.

Oh, darn, either Rob had given her the wrong number or she'd misunderstood him. Now what was she going to do?

Without warning, the door in front of her opened abruptly, and a man came charging out. Not bothering to look up, he careened full force into Lark, knocking her off balance. She gasped, and instinctively her hands flew out in a protective gesture, where the left one was caught as the self-closing door slammed shut.

It all happened in a split second, and Lark screamed as white-hot pain splintered through her. The man's arms grasped her around the waist in an effort to steady them both. "My hand!" she cried, and with a muttered oath he quickly sized up the situation and kicked the door open.

She pulled her hand away and clutched it with her other one in a futile effort to relieve the agony that shot all the way to her shoulder. Her breath came in gasps as tears welled in her green eyes.

"Let me see," the man said, and gently wrapped his fingers around her throbbing wrist. "Good Lord, we'd better get this taken care of."

He still had one arm around her waist and the other hand around her wrist as he led her into the office from which he'd just come. Lark had a hazy pain-filled vision of a woman hurrying across the room. "What happened?" the woman asked, then caught sight of Lark's bruised and rap-

idly swelling hand. She gestured toward a hallway to the left.
"This way," she said, and she led them past more closed
doors and into a bathroom, where she turned on a faucet
and told the man to put Lark's hand under the stream of
cold water.

Lark gasped and a sob shook her, but almost immediately some of the anguish began to recede. The woman left
but soon returned with ice cubes wrapped in a towel.
"Here," she said, and shut off the water, "this improvised
ice pack should be more effective."

By this time Lark was trembling with shock. The man led
her carefully out of the bathroom and back into the outer
office, where he sat her down on a couch. He sat beside her
and positioned her hand while the woman applied the ice.
The soothing cold relieved the tension in Lark, and she sank
back against the comforting chest of the tender stranger, her
cheek pressed into the shoulder of his suit coat. The mate-
rial was a soft, fine-spun wool that caressed her skin.

She knew she shouldn't be cuddling up to a man she'd
never seen before. In fact, with her attention so solidly riv-
eted on the pain in her wrist, she still hadn't really seen him,
but her impression had been one of tall, slender and dark.
She was well aware of his strength, though. She could feel
his muscles underneath his coat, and the scent of him was
tangy and masculine.

He cradled her to him as he would a child who had been
injured, and when he lowered his head and brushed her
forehead with his cheek she realized that he wore a short,
soft beard. "You're shivering," he said, his voice filled with
concern. "I think we'd better take you to a doctor. Do you
have a preference, or shall I drive you to mine?"

He was right, she was shaking uncontrollably, but the ice
had eased the pain in her hand and she was already late for

her appointment with Rob. He'd be wondering what had happened to her.

She leaned back to look up at the man holding her and discovered that he had a square face softened by deep brown hair cut to just above his collar and a close-cropped beard. His coffee-colored eyes brimmed with sympathy and a touch of guilt. "Thank you," she said, and brushed at her tear-stained cheeks with the back of her good hand, "but I'm all right, really. There's no need to see a doctor. My hand's bruised, but nothing seems to be broken." She winced but managed to move her fingers.

"I don't know," he said uncertainly. "Were you coming to see Doug?"

Lark blinked. "Doug?"

"Douglas Caldwell. This is his office, but he won't be in until later."

"Oh. No, I seem to have gotten the wrong address. I was looking for 558 Redwood Avenue."

The man shook his head. "That's two blocks over. This is *Underwood* Avenue. It's a common mistake; the two streets sound so much alike."

"Oh dear." Lark sighed and sat up with the intention of rising, but the man pulled her back against him again.

"No, I'm not going to let you leave here until you stop trembling. Are you driving?"

She nodded, but didn't protest his overruling her. She wasn't sure her legs would hold her if she did stand. Besides, she felt so safe and warm in his arms.

The woman had reseated herself behind the desk and was busy typing. Apparently she was a receptionist or secretary. There had been no designation on the front door as to what sort of business Bishop, Caldwell and Bergen were in, but before Lark could ask, the phone on the desk rang, startling her out of her lethargy.

"I really must be going," she said, and pulled away from the man. This time she did stand, and discovered that her legs were steadier than she had feared.

The man rose also. "I'm afraid I'm going to insist that you see a doctor. After all, I'm the one responsible, and for your protection as well as mine we need a medical opinion. There's a physician's office down the hall. Will he do, or would you prefer someone else?"

Lark knew he was right; she should have a medical opinion. "All right," she said, "but I really am in a hurry. Do you suppose this doctor can see me now?"

"We'll find out." He turned to wave goodbye to the receptionist, who was still talking on the phone, and led Lark out of the office.

The doctor accepted her as an emergency patient, and after a thorough examination of her hand he told her there were no broken bones but to keep it elevated and wrapped in ice. He gave her some pain pills and suggested she see her own physician in the next day or two.

Outside, the man escorted her to her car. "Look," he said anxiously, "I'd feel better if you'd let me drive you home. Where do you live?"

"Oh no, there's no need for that," she assured him. "If you'll just give me directions on how to get to Redwood Avenue I'll be fine. I'm late for an appointment."

He frowned. "Well, if you insist." He didn't sound convinced. "It's only a couple of blocks over and a block down."

He pointed the way to Redwood Avenue and helped her into her car. "I'd really prefer that you let me take you to where you're going. You'll have trouble steering the car with that swollen hand."

She knew he was right, but she couldn't impose on him any longer. "Thanks for your concern," she said, "but please don't blame yourself for this mishap. It was just an unavoidable accident. I don't have far to go, and I promise to keep using ice to bring down the swelling."

He sighed and stepped away. "Okay, if that's the way you want it, but be careful."

"I will," she said, and started the motor.

It wasn't until she'd driven around the corner that she realized they hadn't even exchanged names.

Fifteen minutes later she stood in front of the door marked Carlisle Private Investigations. Thank heaven this time she'd gotten it right. She turned the knob and walked into a reception room much smaller and shabbier than the one she'd just left. It was scrupulously clean and tastefully furnished, however, and the tall, thin woman behind the desk greeted her with a smile. "Please tell me you're Lark Carlisle," she said with a look of mock pleading.

Lark laughed. "Right. Sorry I'm late. Has Rob been wondering what happened to me?"

The secretary grinned. "That's putting it mildly. He's been barking into the intercom every few minutes asking if you're here yet. By the way, I'm Elaine Lester."

She held out a hand and Lark clasped it. "Happy to meet you, Elaine. I got lost and then had a slight accident." She raised her bruised hand.

Just then Rob's voice sounded over the intercom. "Elaine, isn't Lark here *yet?*"

"She just walked in, boss, but you'd better come out here."

She'd hardly straightened up before Rob opened the door to the connecting room and stepped through, closing it behind him. "Lark, where have you—"

His jaw dropped as he caught sight of her purple, swollen hand. "What happened?"

Lark explained to her brother and his secretary the events of the past hour, and after she'd made it plain that she didn't need to go home and lie down but *could* use some more ice, Elaine went to get it for her while Rob briefed her.

"You missed the interview I'd set up for you to listen in on, but I've just started talking to the couple in my office now. I'll take you in and introduce you."

When Elaine came back with the ice pack, Lark followed Rob into the office while excitement and apprehension warred within her. Rob was a private investigator, and he'd agreed to let her work with him on some of his cases during the few weeks she'd be vacationing with him and his family.

Rob's office was larger than the reception room. A bright, cheerful place with wide windows and comfortable furnishings. A room designed to put his clients at ease.

Seated in two wraparound cane-backed chairs in front of the oak desk was a prosperous-looking middle-aged couple who turned toward the door as Rob and Lark entered. The man stood. "Mr. and Mrs. Ulric," Rob said heartily. "I'd like to introduce my sister, Lark Carlisle. She's recently graduated from the University of Arizona and is visiting with us for a while before she starts work on the Phoenix police force. She'll be helping me with some of my cases, and I'd like her to sit in if you don't mind."

Lark smiled and shook hands with the couple, and they indicated that they had no objection to her presence.

"Please, sit down," Rob said, and motioned to a chair in the corner for Lark. When they were all seated he asked, "Now, what can I do for you?"

Frederik Ulric, a short, balding, rotund man in his early sixties, answered. "It's about our daughter, Giselle Ulric Nolan. She disappeared last year during a court battle with her husband, Jonathan Nolan, for custody of their two children and hasn't been heard from since."

Lark's eyebrows rose. This sounded interesting.

"I seem to remember reading something about it at the time," Rob said carefully. "You say Mrs. Nolan is still missing? She didn't take the children with her, did she?"

This time it was Alice Ulric who answered. "No, she didn't, and we haven't heard from our daughter since the day she dropped out of sight. The police won't do a thing about it." Her several chins trembled with emotion.

She dabbed at her faded blue eyes with a handkerchief and settled her generous bulk more comfortably in the chair.

Rob glanced at both of them. "As I remember, Jonathan and Giselle Nolan were divorced and she had custody of the children, then later Jonathan filed suit for physical custody."

"That's right," Frederik said. "He'd tried to take them from her when they were divorced, but the judge let her keep them, and rightly so. She adored her children and she was an excellent mother. Then, a year after the divorce, Jonathan again filed for physical custody, and it was while the case was still being heard that Giselle disappeared. She just dropped off the face of the earth, and none of her family or friends has heard from her since."

Lark adjusted the ice pack on her aching hand and wondered why Mr. Nolan had been so anxious to take the children away from his wife if she was the loving parent that her father portrayed her as.

"I understood that there was a police investigation at that time," Rob remarked.

"There was, but only because *we* filed a missing-persons report, not her ex-husband. Oh no." Frederik was becoming more and more agitated. "He didn't make any effort to find out what had happened to her. He was given custody of the children by default, and he didn't give a damn about the woman who had given birth to them.''

Unable to contain her curiosity, Lark broke in. "What conclusions did the police come to when their investigation was completed?''

Frederik Ulric's round face reddened. "None at all. They asked a few questions, put out a missing-persons report, and closed the case. They had the nerve to tell me that since she was an adult and there was no evidence of foul play there was nothing they could do.''

"That's true," Rob said. "I used to be a police officer, and it was always difficult to explain to family and friends that an adult has a right to drop out of sight if he or she wants to.''

Alice Ulric spoke again, her tone agitated and quarrelsome. "But our daughter wouldn't do that! She'd know how we'd worry. She'd never be so inconsiderate.''

Rob sighed, and Lark empathized with his frustration. He'd heard that argument, almost word for word, hundreds of times during his five years on the Phoenix police force. She knew that she'd say exactly the same thing if someone she loved had disappeared, but the fact remained that most adults who vanish do so because they don't want to be found. The majority of them eventually come home and try to make peace with their families.

"What is it you want of me?" Rob asked.

"We want you to find our daughter," Frederik answered.

"Have you any idea where I might start looking?''

"Yes, start with her husband.'' Alice's voice was hoarse with bitterness.

"Do you have reason to think he knows where she is?''

"Of course he knows where she is!" Frederik rose heavily from the chair and glared across the desk at Rob. "He's the one who got rid of her."

Lark gasped, and the shock of Frederik's words brought Rob to his feet. "Now wait a minute. Are you insinuating that Jonathan Nolan—"

"I'm not insinuating anything." Frederik's heavy muscular legs were planted wide apart, and his fists clenched and unclenched at his sides. "I'm telling you that Jonathan wanted those children and he was about to lose the second custody hearing. That's a fact. He couldn't prove that Giselle was an unfit mother because she wasn't. His case against her was falling apart—even the newspaper commented on it—and it was right at that time when she disappeared. You bet your life Jonathan Nolan had something to do with it. He drove her away, and I want to know what he did to her."

Excitement built in Lark. This case had all the elements of a real thriller. Too bad she wasn't a writer.

Alice opened her purse and extracted a handkerchief that she touched to the corners of her eyes. "Our poor little granddaughters need their mother. Why, they don't even have a housekeeper anymore. The last one quit a month ago and they haven't been able to find another one, so now there's nobody to look after them."

Rob frowned. "I understood that the oldest girl is a teenager."

"That's right," Alice admitted, "but Patricia's only three, and it's not fair for Candace to have full responsibility for the baby now that school's out for the summer. Candace needs her vacation and Patty needs her mother."

Rob asked a few more questions, then told the Ulrics he'd look into it and let them know if he felt he could be of any help.

After they left, Lark was bursting with questions. "Are you going to take the case, Rob? It sounds exciting."

Lark had moved to one of the chairs the Ulrics had been using, and she watched the indecision flicker across her brother's face. "I'm not sure," he said.

She was puzzled. "But why not? They seem to have a legitimate problem."

"I'm familiar with the case. For that matter, so is all of Eureka. Jonathan and Giselle Nolan had been the subject of polite gossip among the citizens of the community for years. Their marital problems were no secret, thanks to Giselle and her runaway tongue. I know Jonathan Nolan well enough to be almost positive that he had nothing to do with his wife's disappearance and if he knew where she was he'd tell her parents."

"*Almost* positive?" Lark asked.

Rob shrugged. "Jonathan's not a personal friend; I know him through business associations. His family's been in the lumber business in Eureka for generations. He's been head of it since his father died six years ago, and I've never met a person who didn't like him. Even his competitors admit that he's fair and honest and has a damn good head on his shoulders. I'm as sure of him as it's possible to be of another person."

Lark nodded. "In that case, wouldn't it be better for you to find his wife and put an end to the speculation of his in-laws?"

Rob tapped the eraser end of a pencil on the desk. "Yes, it would, and that's the only reason I'm even considering it. The Ulrics are a power to be reckoned with in this town. He's president of our largest bank, and she's one of our most influential social leaders. The best course of action would be to plant a woman in Nolan's home as a housekeeper, but I'd have to bring in someone from out of town. Jonathan would probably recognize any of my staff."

The same thought had occurred to Lark, and she was bubbling with excitement. "Rob, let me do it. I've got a degree in criminal justice, and no one in Eureka knows me. It could be months before there's an opening on the police academy back home, and meanwhile I could be getting some experience. If I'm living in his home with his family, it shouldn't take long to find out whether or not Jonathan Nolan is involved in his wife's disappearance."

Her eyes sparkled as she practically bounced in her chair. "Oh please, Rob, say yes!"

He frowned and continued tapping the desk with the pencil. "Let me think about it," he finally said, and looked at his watch. "We'd better get going. Melanie's expecting us home for lunch."

Lark knew it would do no good to try to rush him into giving her an answer. Rob was methodical and wouldn't be stampeded.

Rob's home was one of the remodeled old ornate Victorians so prevalent in Eureka, a legacy from the lumber barons of the 1800s. His pretty, dark-haired wife, Melanie, and their two preschool-age sons kept the simple meal lively and fun, but when Melanie excused herself to put the children down for their naps, Rob poured more coffee into his and Lark's mugs. "So, how goes it with you, honey?" he asked. "We did a lot of talking last night when you arrived, but it was mostly superficial. I want to know about the real you. Sorry we weren't able to attend your graduation, but we're awfully proud of you. I hope you know that."

Lark nodded and smiled. "I know, and I understand why you couldn't be there. I'm glad now that you couldn't. It gave me a good excuse to come up here and visit you while

I'm waiting to hear about an opening at the police academy."

"Our little Lark, a police officer," he mused. "I'll bet Dad's popping buttons all over the place. It's no small thing to pass all those exams with such high scores." His voice was filled with pride.

Lark lowered her eyes in embarrassment. "Thank you, and yes, Dad is proud. Almost as proud as he was when you passed the exams with even higher scores. If his heart hadn't forced him to take a disability retirement he'd still be a captain on the force. He misses it—and he misses you, Rob. Even though he and Mom come up here for a visit at least once a year, it's not the same."

Rob sighed. "I know. I don't suppose he'll ever totally forgive me for resigning from the force to start my own investigative agency."

Lark leaned forward in her chair. "That's not true. He was disappointed, but he's never held it against you."

Rob shifted uncomfortably and hesitated before speaking again. "Lark, how are you, really? Do you ever see Wayne Bancroft?"

She'd known that question was coming, and she answered it with ease. "Yes, I see him now and then. We live in the same city, and we still have some of the same friends. He and Samantha were married as soon as our divorce was final, and they seem happy."

"And you?" Rob probed. "Are you happy, Lark?"

She settled back and sighed. "I'm fine, honest. I thought my life had ended when Wayne told me he'd fallen in love with another woman and wanted a divorce, but enrolling in college was the best thing that could have happened to me. It gave me something else to think about, and I have my degree now and I will never again have to rely on a man."

Rob swore. "You're more forgiving than I am. If I ever get my hands on that son of a—"

"Don't, Rob," Lark pleaded. "It's all in the past, and I seldom think about it anymore. Actually, Wayne did me a favor by walking out. I never should have married at eighteen. I was too young, and except for the passion that we mistook for love, we were totally incompatible. Two years of living together taught us that much. It's better this way, believe me."

She took a swallow of her hot coffee, then got right to the point. "Okay, brother mine, let's stop beating around the bush. Are you going to let me work with you on the Nolan case?"

Two days later, clutching a clearly marked map of the city, Lark headed her Mustang in the direction of the Nolan residence. When she'd phoned the number given in the classified ad section of the newspaper the day before, she'd talked to the eldest daughter, who told her to come for an interview anytime before noon on Saturday.

She and Rob had invented a fictitious background and a motive for her seeking a job as a housekeeper, and she was dressed in what she hoped was the proper outfit to wear when applying for a domestic position—a skirt and blouse with a hand-knit cardigan to ward off the chill of temperatures in the high sixties.

The Nolan home was newer and larger than she'd expected. It set toward the back of a large lot and was built of redwood, brick and glass. Lark turned into the curved driveway and parked her shabby car beneath a towering elm tree. A stab of doubt disturbed her.

Had she been wrong to argue so eagerly with Rob for this assignment? She'd thought he was just being overly protective of his little sister when he insisted that she wasn't ex-

erienced enough to handle it, but now she wondered. She'd
always been an essentially honest person. The few times in
er life that she'd tried to lie she'd been so flustered that
obody had believed her. She couldn't allow that to hap-
en this time. It would reflect badly on Rob and the agency.

No, she'd gotten herself into this and it was too late for
econd thoughts now.

She had straightened her shoulders and started up the
walkway when a huge blond dog came loping around the
ide of the house, barking at one end and wagging his bushy
ail at the other. He screeched to a halt in front of her and
at on her feet with his tongue hanging out.

Lark laughed and reached down to pet the friendly animal. "Hi there," she said, and scratched behind his ears,
much to his canine delight. "I do have an appointment, you
know," she told him, "so if you'd kindly get off my feet, I'd
ike to speak to your master."

The dog looked at her adoringly for a moment, then got
up and led the way to the massive hand-carved double
loors. She pushed the doorbell and heard the sound of
himes inside. Classy.

She had just raised her hand to push the button again
when one of the doors opened and the figure of a man
locked the entrance. Lark stared. He was tall and slender,
ut well-toned muscles were visible in his arms and chest
under a close-fitting T-shirt and in his thighs beneath tight
eans. His dark eyes were wide with surprise; his squarish
ace was framed by deep brown hair and a short beard, and
oth were threaded with gray, which she hadn't noticed be-
ore.

It was the man she'd collided with in the office building
on Underwood Avenue. The one who'd tended her bruised
and with so much gentleness and caring, and who had
aunted her dreams ever since!

Chapter Two

Jonathan Nolan blinked, then blinked again, as he stared at the incredibly beautiful young lady standing on his door step. When the bell chimed, he'd assumed it to be the appli cant for the housekeeping position. Instead it was th woman who'd caught her hand in the door of Doug Cald well's office on Thursday. The phantom woman he hadn' been able to get out of his thoughts since. He could still fee her softly curved body against his; he'd been feeling it eve since she'd driven away and left him standing at the cur yearning to run after her.

She was dressed differently. Thursday she'd been wear ing a navy blue suit and had looked like a very young busi nesswoman. Today she resembled a college girl, dressed i a dark rose skirt and blouse that clung to her full breasts an the tantalizing flare of her hips. The color accentuated the healthy glow of her creamy complexion and the startlin green of her almond-shaped eyes. He knew from th shocked look in those eyes that she was as surprised as he.

Before he could find his voice she spoke. "Jonathan No-
an?"

She knew his name, so he must be mistaken. This wasn't
bizarre coincidence. She'd learned his name and come to
e him. But why?

He nodded and made a massive effort to pull himself to-
ether. "Yes, I'm Jonathan Nolan," he finally managed to
ay. "Won't you come in?"

He stepped back to let her pass and caught a whiff of the
lusive scent—a combination of bath soap and apple blos-
oms—that he'd noticed about her when she'd cuddled
gainst him and sobbed.

Stop that, dammit, he admonished himself. He was be-
aving like a first-class idiot. Besides, if she'd taken the
rouble to find out who he was and come to his house, it
robably meant she blamed him for the accident and in-
ended to sue. A quick glance at her hand confirmed that it
vas still bruised and slightly swollen.

He led the way down the short hall to the living room.
"Please, sit down." He motioned to a blue velvet chair, then
eated himself on the matching couch. "Now, perhaps
ou'll tell me your name and what I can do for you."

The surprised look in her exotic eyes intensified. "I'm
Lark Car—Bancroft," she stammered. "I called about the
ousekeeping position."

Lark's first impulse when she'd realized that the man who
ad been constantly in her thoughts for the past few days
vas actually Jonathan Nolan, the person she was investi-
ating, had been to turn and run. It was only through sheer
villpower that she'd managed to stand there quietly until
he'd regained enough composure to speak. Now she'd almost blown it by calling herself Carlisle instead of Bancroft, the name she'd used when she was married. Rob had
uggested she introduce herself as Lark Bancroft to keep

Jonathan from connecting her with Carlisle Private Investigations.

Jonathan looked stunned. "*You* want to work as my
housekeeper?"

She nodded, hoping to give herself time to collect her
scattered thoughts. "Yes. No. I mean, I'm applying for the
job, but I had no idea you were the man who ran the ad."

"You're not exactly the housekeeper type," he said dryly.
"Besides, you can't work at much of anything with your
hand still swollen and sore. Did you have an X ray? Was
there any serious damage?"

"Yes, I did, and no, it's not seriously injured." She held
up her hand and wiggled all her fingers. "See, I can use it
quite well, and what exactly is a 'housekeeper type'?"

He frowned. "You know what I mean. You're much too
young and pretty—and, I suspect, intelligent—to work as a
housekeeper. I need somebody middle-aged and motherly.
I have two daughters, one a preschooler who needs constant
care."

"Just what do my age and looks have to do with the kind
of care I can give your house and children?" she snapped,
then drew a deep breath and launched into the story she and
Rob had fabricated. "I'm twenty-five years old and recently divorced. I want to work as a housekeeper because it
will give me board and room and an income while I go to
school. I plan to enroll at Humbolt State University this fall
and get a degree so I won't have to be a domestic worker all
my life."

She hadn't lied about her age or marital status, and as for
the made-up plans for schooling, she wouldn't be there long
enough to have to worry about carrying them out.

"Don't you have family or friends you can live with?" he
asked.

She shook her head. "Not here. I'm from Phoenix, Arizona, but I wanted to get away after my husband and I—" She choked on the lie and couldn't go on. This was going to be more difficult than she'd imagined.

"Why did you come to Eureka?" Jonathan asked. "I would have thought you'd choose Los Angeles or San Francisco. We're not exactly an exciting area."

Lark had her story memorized. "We used to camp up here in the redwoods while I was growing up. I've always loved it, and once I was free to live anywhere I wanted I decided the ocean would be a nice change from the desert. Besides, Humbolt State is a great place to study forestry."

"Forestry?" Jonathan's look was one of disbelief. "You're full of surprises. What's wrong with being a model, or a secretary, or maybe a teacher?"

Lark gritted her teeth and forced herself to speak calmly. "Not a thing. If you're so interested in those professions, why didn't you study for one of them?"

His startled look told her she'd made her point. "Touché," he said after a moment. "I guess I sounded like a bit of a chauvinist."

"A bit," she said, and grinned.

"I can only plead confusion," he replied. "You look and act so feminine—" He held up his hand as her eyes widened with anger. "I know, I know, you can be a park ranger and still be feminine, but you'll have to admit that you look more like a photographer's model."

She relaxed and smiled, but she wondered what he'd say if he knew she'd been trained as a peace officer. He obviously meant well, and she couldn't afford to antagonize him. She had to get this job. "Thank you," she said. "I can't think of any woman who wouldn't be flattered to hear that she looks like a model, but I'm afraid I'm a little too, uh, curvy for that profession."

His gaze roamed over her, admiring but not undressing. "Then there's something wrong with the profession's standards," he said, then cleared his throat and looked away from her. "Actually, your looks are one reason why I can't consider hiring you as a housekeeper."

Lark straightened. "I beg your pardon?"

"Oh, come on now," he said impatiently. "I'm twelve years older than you, but that doesn't make me elderly. I'm as susceptible to desirable women as the next man, and I don't need the frustration of having one who's off limits living in my own home. Besides, you must know the kind of talk that would cause."

She hadn't thought of that, but then, she hadn't known that Jonathan Nolan would be so young and handsome. "But that's ridiculous," she protested. "You have two daughters who live here too."

His bark of laughter was more derisive than happy. "You can't be that naive. You've been married; you must know that children in the house aren't going to inhibit a red-blooded male when he wants a woman."

His words touched off an answering chord in her that made her squirm, and she was aware that she was blushing like a schoolgirl. The thought of him coming to her bed in the middle of the night was alarmingly appealing. Good heavens, she hadn't been seriously tempted by a man since her divorce. If she was smart, she'd tell Jonathan Nolan goodbye and leave. After all, he was suspected of being responsible for his ex-wife's disappearance!

Unfortunately, the combination of his charisma and her desire to protect Rob's professional reputation was more persuasive than her good sense. She lowered her head, hoping he wouldn't see the telltale blush. "It won't work, you know," she said quietly.

"What won't work?"

"Your attempt to scare me away. I know you're an honorable man. I did some checking before I applied for this position, and everyone agreed on that point. I don't believe for a moment that you'd take me by force. Even if you were suddenly overcome by lust—which we both know isn't going to happen—you wouldn't do anything like that with your daughters in the house."

She could see that she'd caught him off guard, and she settled back in her chair. "Now, tell me what's really bothering you."

He looked thoroughly rattled, but he quickly regained his composure. "I can see I've underestimated you, Lark," he said thoughtfully, "but you've also underestimated your appeal, and that's a dangerous thing to do."

He settled himself more comfortably on the sofa. "Okay, I'll stipulate that you'd be safe living here with me, but that doesn't eliminate the probability of gossip and speculation. You're too young and attractive, and I don't want that sort of talk."

He was putting up barriers that were hard to knock down. It *was* a sticky situation, but one she'd have to overcome somehow if she was going to do her job. "Look," she said, playing it by ear as she went along, "I can cook, clean, and I'm good with children. Also, your golden retriever likes me."

"That stupid dog likes everyone," Jonathan muttered.

Lark ignored his comment as she continued. "It's awkward if you don't have a wife, but that's all the more reason why you need me. In case you didn't know, housekeepers are in scarce supply."

"Tell me about it," he said sarcastically. "I've been advertising for weeks. So far the applicants have been either teenagers or elderly ladies hoping to supplement their social security."

"Then you've finally found a nice middle ground." She beamed triumphantly. "I'm neither an adolescent nor a senior citizen. Won't you at least introduce me to your children and see if they approve?"

He sighed and rose to his feet. "I guess I don't have much choice," he said as he headed out of the room. "Excuse me, I'll go round them up."

He called to the girls as he disappeared around a corner, and Lark was left alone.

Her gaze moved over the room. It was large, decorated in shades of blue and sand, with original oil paintings on the walls. The back wall was all windows that started about four feet from the floor and rose to just below the ceiling. Sheer sand-colored panel curtains covered the wall from ceiling to floor, with blue patterned draperies at either end. Lark got up and walked over to look out. The view was breathtaking. The house was situated on a cliff that overlooked Humbolt Bay, and the blue water with its white foamy breakers lapped at the rocks below. She could hear the muted roar of the ocean as it hurled itself against the clean washed stone, then retreated and again started its rush to shore.

She was still standing there when Jonathan came back with his daughters. He introduced the pretty teenager with mahogany hair and matching eyes as Candace, and the preschooler with wheat-colored curls and brown eyes as Patricia. Lark smiled and offered her hand to Candace, who took it in a firm grip. "Candace is a lovely name," Lark said. "Are you ever called Candy?"

The girl shook her head. "No, I don't like it. It sounds too babyish."

Lark turned to the little one, who was being held in her father's arms. "Good morning, Patricia." She stroked a shock of damp curls off the child's forehead. She was warm and sleepy-eyed and wearing pink pajamas. "I'll bet you just woke up."

The little girl hid her face in her daddy's shoulder, and Lark looked at Jonathan over the curly head. "I'm sorry. I didn't realize she was asleep. I didn't mean for you to waken her."

"She was awake," he said. "Besides, it's time she got up. If she sleeps too long in the morning she doesn't want to nap in the afternoon, and then she's fussy before bedtime. Shall we all sit down?"

He strode across the room and seated himself once more on the sofa with Patricia in his lap. Candace sat beside them, and Lark resumed her seat in the chair.

Jonathan took charge of the conversation. "Girls, Mrs. Bancroft has offered to be our new housekeeper."

Instinctively Lark opened her mouth to correct him on her name, then remembered that she was again using it and remained silent.

Candace was the first to speak. "But she doesn't look like a housekeeper!"

Lark drew a frustrated breath. Apparently this was going to be a real problem. She should have tried to look older, more matronly.

She smiled at Candace. "I'm sorry I don't look the part," she said, keeping her tone light, "but I've been cooking and keeping house for seven years now, and I'm really very good at it."

Jonathan eyed her speculatively. "You must have been awfully young when you married."

"I was eighteen," she replied, then turned her attention to Candace, whom she judged to be fifteen or sixteen. "I was too young, and the marriage proved to be a mistake. I'm divorced now, and that's why I'm applying for work as a housekeeper. I haven't been trained to do anything else."

She hoped Candace would remember her words and learn from them. Too many young girls thought it was the badge of an adult to get married right out of high school. Often, it only proved how immature they were. At least Lark had had the good sense not to start a family.

Candace looked thoughtful. "Yeah," she said. "My mom was married when she was eighteen, and she and Dad are divorced too."

Lark expected Jonathan to intervene, but he remained silent, leaving her to grapple for an answer. "It's better for young people to wait until they're older, more mature, before entering into anything as deeply committing as marriage. I'm sorry now that I didn't go on to college and finish my education after high school. Every girl should be trained to support herself, and not have to rely on someone else to do it for her."

She was speaking from the heart. For some reason it was important to her that Jonathan Nolan's daughter not make the same mistake she herself had made.

"Why didn't you go to college after you were married? My mother did."

This time Jonathan did try to interrupt, but Lark stopped him. "No, please, Mr. Nolan," she said, "I don't mind answering."

She turned her attention to Candace. "I couldn't go to college because I had to work and support us so my husband could get his degree. He was studying to be a lawyer, and it was very expensive. I cleaned people's houses, and I was paid well." She gave a bitter laugh. "You'd be surprised how much people are willing to pay someone else to do the dirty work for them. So you see, I've had experience as a housekeeper."

Everything she'd told the child was the truth. She just neglected to mention that her marriage had only lasted for couple of years, and that after that she had cleaned other people's houses to put herself through college while her husband finished law school on his second wife's money.

Lark shifted to look at the toddler, still sitting quietly on her father's lap. "How about you, buttercup?" she said with a grin. "Do you have any comments?"

The youngster eyed her unsmilingly. "Not buttercup," she said slowly. "Patty."

She was an appealing child, and Lark longed to hold her, but she was afraid she'd frighten her if she suggested it. "Patty!" she exclaimed. "What a pretty name. How old are you, Patty?"

The little girl held up the fingers of one small hand. "This many."

"One, two, three," Lark counted, reaching over to each little finger as she did. "That's a nice age to be. I bet you'll be starting school pretty soon."

Patty stuck two of her fingers in her mouth and settled back against her daddy, obviously not interested in continuing the conversation.

"She's been in a day care center for the past month," Jonathan said. "When our housekeeper left I had no choice, but I'd prefer to keep her here at home—although I wouldn't mind letting her go to day care two or three mornings a week." His eyes met Lark's. "That's why I'm so particular about whom I hire as a housekeeper. She'll have to look after Patty during the day while I'm gone."

It pleased Lark that Jonathan was so concerned about his little daughter. That there was a strong bond between the two was evident in the way Patty curled up in her father's arms so trustingly. Candace seemed content, too. There was none of the tension between father and daughter that was so often present with teenagers. Lark had only been in his house for less than an hour, but she had an intuitive feeling

that Jonathan Nolan was a loving parent who would always put his children's welfare before his own.

So why had he been so desperate to take them away from
their mother?

"I'm sure Patty and I would get along well together," she
said in answer to his remark. "I have a couple of little
nephews about her age."

She knew immediately that she had made a mistake.

"Tell us about your background," Jonathan said. "Do
you have brothers and sisters?"

Lark bit her lip and wished she'd never brought up the
subject. "Ye-e-es," she said reluctantly. "I have two
brothers. My mother's an ornithologist and my dad's retired." She hoped he wouldn't ask what her dad was retired
from.

Fortunately he seemed more interested in her mother's
profession. "An ornithologist? The study of birds. So that's
the reason she named you Lark."

She chuckled. "That's right. My brothers are Robin and
Jay."

Jonathan laughed, and it was a strong, happy sound. "I
imagine Robin would have preferred something like Hawk."

"Robin would have preferred almost anything else," she
said, remembering Rob's embarrassment the few times
people found out his full name.

"Are your brothers older or younger than you?"

"One older and one younger. Robin's the one who's given
me nephews, and Jay's a senior in high school."

"And they all live in Phoenix." It was more a statement
rather than a question.

"Yes." Lark pushed back her interfering conscience. He
hadn't asked specifically if Rob lived in Phoenix; he'd simply assumed, and she hadn't corrected him.

"We were in Phoenix once." It was Candace who spoke. "Remember, Dad? It was so hot that I got sick, and Mom got mad because I upchucked..."

Her voice trailed off to an uneasy silence as she apparently realized she was telling things that shouldn't be shared with strangers.

Jonathan rescued her. "Yes, I remember. It was wrong of me to insist on taking my family with me on that business trip. The heat is too intense for a little girl who's lived all her life in our cool, foggy climate."

Lark felt a wave of admiration for this man who put the blame on himself rather than let his daughter be embarrassed or his ex-wife be shown in a negative light.

Out of the corner of her eye she saw Jonathan glance at his watch, and with a sinking feeling she realized that she had probably overstayed her welcome. She jumped up and hooked the long straps of her purse over her shoulder. "Well," she said brightly, "it's been a pleasure meeting all of you, but I really must run."

Jonathan sat Patty on the sofa beside him and stood. "Must you leave?" he asked. "I promised to take the girls to Sequoia Park today. You're welcome to come along if you'd like."

Lark could hardly believe what she was hearing. He was inviting her along on a family outing. Did that mean he'd changed his mind about hiring her?

"Sequoia Park?" She'd never heard of it.

He nodded. "It's a fifty-acre grove of virgin redwoods that house our zoo."

"How marvelous." Her enthusiasm was genuine. "I'd love to go—that is, if it's all right with the girls."

She looked at Candace, who replied, "Sure. Wait till you see the bear cubs. They're so cute and cuddly."

"Then it's settled," Jonathan said. "Candace, you get Patty dressed while I fix her some breakfast."

Candace took Patty by the hand and led her up the stairs while Jonathan turned toward the kitchen. "May I help?" Lark asked as she followed after him.

"There's not much to do—" he slowed so she could catch up. "—but you can have a cup of coffee and talk to me."

The kitchen was large and thoroughly modern, with custom-made hardwood cabinets and brick walls. A room any woman would love. "Oh, what a beautiful kitchen," she said eagerly as her gaze roamed over it. "It would be a joy to work in."

"Yes," he agreed, "if you like to cook, which is not my favorite pastime." He ran water into a bright red tea kettle and set it on the stove.

"Look, I'd be happy to fix breakfast for Patty," Lark offered.

Jonathan turned and looked at her. "Thanks, but I'm only going to make instant oatmeal and toast. The mugs are in the cupboard to your right."

She found the mugs, tan with a pattern of red strawberries and green leaves, and filled them from the electric coffeemaker, then pulled the plug and handed him one. They sat at the round oak table in the corner, and he reached for her injured hand and held it in the palm of his. "It still looks awfully sore," he said.

His own hand was large and warm, rough and callused in places, but his touch was gentle, and his dark eyes brimmed with sympathy.

She couldn't seem to pull her gaze away. "It's not, really." Her voice was low and a little breathless. "It only hurts when I forget and try to pick something up with it."

The fingers of his other hand moved tenderly over the harsh purple bruises. "I can't tell you how sorry I am."

"Oh, but it wasn't your fault," she hastened to assure him. "It was strictly an accident."

"I should have been more careful when I tore out of Doug's office. He's my attorney and I'd dropped by to see him, but apparently he'd been going down in one elevator while I was coming up in the other. We'd just missed each other, and I was hoping to catch up with him before he got away."

Somehow during their exchange of words they had leaned closer to one another, so that now their faces were only inches apart, close enough for Lark to see the tiny lines at the corners of his eyes and to feel his warm breath on her cheek. "Then I'm the one who's sorry," she said huskily. "I shouldn't have been standing in front of the door like that. I'd just realized that I must have had the wrong address, and I was wondering what to do next when the door opened and we collided."

For a moment neither of them spoke, and the silence was charged with emotion. Slowly he raised her hand to his lips and kissed the darkest bruise, then rubbed it carefully against the softness of his short beard in a caress that made her tingle all the way to her toes. She breathed a soft moan and started to raise her other hand to return the caress, when a sharp whistle exploded through the room, making them both jump apart. The water had come to a boil in the tea kettle.

Sequoia Park was a veritable paradise for animal lovers. Besides the main zoo, the bear grotto, and the deer and elk paddocks, there was a petting zoo with tame young animals that the children could pet. Patty loved it, and she hugged the little deer and piglets and alpaca llamas to her with joyous abandon. She handed each in turn to Lark, who cuddled them before turning them over to Candace. Jonathan leaned back against the fence and watched with a smile as Lark played with his daughters and the baby animals.

"You'd never work out as my housekeeper," he teased her when she brought over one of the lambs to show how it would suck from a bottle of milk for her. "I'd get you mixed up with the kids and insist that your dates bring you home by ten on weeknights. I'm inclined to be overprotective of my daughters. Just ask Candace."

In light of the electricity that crackled between them when they got close, Lark considered it highly unlikely that he'd ever mistake her for a daughter, but she grinned and played along. "Yes, Daddy, just so long as you don't insist on chaperoning."

He reached out and swatted her playfully. "Keep a civil tongue in your head, child, or that's exactly what I'll do."

By the time they'd stopped at a fast-food place and bought hamburgers to take home for a late lunch, Lark was both happy and confident. Happy because she'd had such a great time romping around the park with Jonathan and his daughters, and confident because she had every reason to be. It hadn't taken them but minutes to get on a first-name basis, and the girls liked her. Candace had teased and laughed with her, and on the way home Patty had curled up on Lark's lap and almost fallen asleep. After less than four hours the girls were at ease with her. She was sure they'd accept her as their housekeeper and baby-sitter.

There didn't seem to be any doubt but that Jonathan approved of her. She'd been aware of his purpose in taking her on the outing with them, and she'd made a special effort to show him how well she could get along with his children, and how much she enjoyed them. He'd stood back and watched and seemed to approve.

There was a strong attraction between them. She felt it, and she knew he did too. Although he hadn't touched her again, after they'd been interrupted by the singing tea kettle, she knew that the awareness she felt for him was reciprocated, and she tingled with pleasure. Now she had an added reason for wanting to work for Jonathan Nolan. Not only was she anxious to prove that he had nothing to do with his wife's disappearance, but she wanted to get to know him better. Much better.

Lark had dated frequently since her divorce, but never had she cared enough for a man to go beyond the usual good-night kiss. Some of her frustrated dates called her a tease, but it wasn't that. She'd been so sure that she was in love with Wayne Bancroft that she'd defied both of her parents and Rob to marry him two months after she'd graduated from high school. When he left her for another woman it had done terrible things to her belief in herself as a desirable woman. She wasn't going to be hurt that badly again, and she'd made sure of it by never letting another man get that close to her.

Jonathan Nolan hadn't asked permission; he'd simply slammed into her life and embedded himself in her nervous system. From the first time he'd held her, after the door had closed on her hand, she'd known he was special. Without her ever willing it or wanting it, he'd imprinted himself on her awareness and refused to be shaken off.

He wasn't impervious to her, either. He'd admitted as much that morning when he'd told her it was the reason he couldn't hire her as a housekeeper. Of course, the attraction probably wasn't as strong as he'd led her to believe, but it was uncomfortable enough that his first inclination was to send her away. He hadn't, though. He'd taken her with him on a family outing, and he'd enjoyed the time spent with her. He'd relaxed and romped with the rest of them in the park, and now he was sitting across from her in his kitchen eating hamburgers and french fries and laughing over something Candace had said.

Lark was sure he would tell her she could work for him.

Patty was nodding sleepily in her chair by the time they'd finished their meal, and Lark touched Jonathan's arm to get his attention. She tipped her head toward the child. "I don't think you're going to have to worry about Patty not napping this afternoon. Do you mind if I put her to bed?"

Jonathan pushed back his chair and stood. "Her bedroom's upstairs. Better let me carry her; she's not as lightweight as she looks."

He had picked up the little girl and was starting out of the room with Lark beside him, when Candace spoke. "Dad, can I go over to Maribeth's?"

Jonathan turned to look at her. "Okay, you can take the Toyota, but be back in time to help me fix dinner."

She jumped up, all smiles, and kissed him on the cheek. "Thanks, Dad," she said. "See you later, Lark," she called as she raced out the back door.

"I hope so," Lark yelled, then hurried along with Jonathan. "How long has she been driving?" Lark asked.

"She got her license on her sixteenth birthday, four months ago. She wants me to buy her a car, but I don't go for that. She's too young. I can keep better control if she's driving one of mine."

They started up the stairs. "You sound like my dad. He wouldn't let me have my own car, either. Said he'd seen too many kids get into trouble because of driving high-powered cars with no supervision."

"Your dad's a smart man. What line of work was he in before he retired?"

Lark's mouth opened, then snapped shut. Oh damn, now she'd really done it. She didn't want to mention that there were police officers in her family. It might make him suspicious of her if somehow he were to find out that his in-laws were having him investigated. When was she going to learn not to talk so much?

She preferred not to say anything rather than lie to this man who was suddenly so important to her.

Fortunately, they entered Patty's room just then, and she changed the subject by commenting on it. It was a little girl's dream room decorated in shades of pink and cream, and the furniture was white with gold trim. Toys and clothes were scattered around in a manner that told better than words of their need for a housekeeper.

Jonathan laid the sleepy youngster in the unmade crib, and Lark removed her shoes and socks and slid her under the covers. Lark leaned over and kissed the warm little cheek, then stood and waited while Jonathan did the same.

Back downstairs, Lark headed for the kitchen and began cleaning up the clutter they'd made with their take-out food. She was already starting to feel at home in this beautiful house. Jonathan needed a housekeeper, the girls needed a substitute mother, and she needed this job. It was all going to work out beautifully.

Jonathan came up behind her. "Don't bother with that, Lark," he said. "We've imposed on you enough today. I'm sure you have other things to do."

"Oh no," she said, and turned to look at him. "I—"

He wasn't smiling as she'd expected. His expression was stern and brooked no argument. Her own smile disappeared as she stammered, "I—I'd be happy to help you straighten up." Her tongue nervously outlined her full lips.

Jonathan's gaze followed the path of her tongue, but his tone was final. "No, Lark. The girls and I have enjoyed your company very much, but I meant what I said earlier. I can't hire you as my live-in housekeeper."

Lark felt as if she'd been slapped. "But why?" Her voice was little more than a whisper. "Candace and Patty like me, and I'd take good care of them."

Jonathan shook his head and looked away from her. "I know you would. I can't hope to find anyone who would be better with them. But my original objection still stands. You're too young to live with me in this house with no other adult present. It would cause nothing but trouble."

Chapter Three

Lark paced the floor of Rob's living room as she re-
counted the day's events to him. "I was shocked," she said
passionately. "I was so sure that he'd decided to hire me."
Her shoulders slumped, and she exhaled slowly. "After that
there was nothing I could do but say goodbye and leave. I'm
sorry, Rob. I let you down."

Rob, who had been sitting on the sofa with his wife, Melanie, stood and patted Lark on the shoulder. "It's not your
fault, honey. You can't help it if you're too sexy to be a
housekeeper." There was laughter in his tone, and she
looked up to see amusement crinkling the corners of his hazel eyes.

"Actually," he continued, "it's my fault. If you'd been
anyone but my little sister I'd have realized that you're too
young and desirable to be living with Jonathan Nolan without a chaperon. I guess men don't think of their sisters as
temptresses. My only thought was that he would be happy
to hire anyone as capable as you."

Melanie spoke from her seat on the sofa. "Really, Rob, I'm afraid you've been married too long." Her tone showed dry amusement.

Rob grinned. "We'll debate that tonight in the privacy o our bedroom. Meanwhile, I think Lark needs a drink, and I know I do. Why don't you ladies entertain each other while I go fix them? Are Manhattans all right?"

Both Melanie and Lark nodded, and Lark sank down wearily in a lounge chair by the fireplace. She ran her fingers through her shoulder-length brown hair and tossed i back from her face. "Honest, Melanie, I feel like such a failure. The first time I get a chance to use my training I flub it."

"Face facts, Lark," Melanie said, "Jonathan's right. He's a man who's been married and had a wife at his disposal, so to speak. Now he's single, but he still has the same needs and desires. I suspect there are a lot of undercurrents flowing between you two, and he's not about to place himself in the agonizing position of being constantly aroused by you and unable to do anything about it."

The heat that flowed through Lark at Melanie's words brought a flush to her creamy complexion. "Really, Melanie," she said, more harshly than she'd intended. "You make it sound so clinical."

"It is clinical. Sex without love isn't lovemaking, and Jonathan is too nice a man to hire a woman as a housekeeper and then seduce her just to relieve his frustration. He's one of the most eligible bachelors in this town, and there are women here who would line up to go to bed with him. He doesn't need the sort of temptation hiring you would provoke."

Fortunately Rob came back with the drinks before Lark had to answer.

It was three days later, on Tuesday morning, that Lark answered the phone while Melanie was vacuuming the upstairs rooms. She immediately recognized the baritone voice at the other end. "Jonathan. How nice to hear from you."

Thank heaven she'd been the one to answer the phone. The day Lark had phoned the Nolan residence to make an appointment for an interview, she'd given Candace Rob's number. What could he want of her now?

"I enjoy talking to you, too," he answered, and there was an undertone to his words that sent shivers down her spine. "I'm afraid I've placed myself in an embarrassing position, and I'm hoping you'll come to my rescue."

"I'll be happy to if I can," she said, her bafflement evident in her tone.

"Don't be too sure." He sounded grim. "After I was so vehement about not hiring you as my housekeeper, I wouldn't blame you if you let me stew in my own juices."

Lark snapped to attention. Was it possible he'd reconsidered?

"I won't try to explain in depth," he continued. "It's too complicated. But I'm a member of a national committee of lumbermen who have been trying to set up a conference with the Chinese authorities to talk about eliminating tariffs so that the United States can export more lumber to their country. They've been putting us off for months, but I've just learned that they've finally agreed and set a date. Unfortunately, we'll have to leave tomorrow if we're going to arrive in time, and I'm desperate. I need someone to stay with Candace and Patty. They have grandparents living in town, but the Ulrics left yesterday on a cruise to Alaska. I can't leave them alone, and I wouldn't want to trust them to a stranger even if I could find someone on such short notice." His frantic concern vibrated over the lines.

"I need you, Lark. I'll pay anything you ask if you'll just move in here until I get back. The girls know and like you, and you're the only person I'd feel comfortable leaving them with while I'm out of the country."

Lark was elated. Not only would she get to know both him and his daughters better, but she could also do some investigating. Check with neighbors and friends, and question Candace. It would have to be handled very subtly, of course, but she could find out a great deal for Rob while she was there.

No sense in sounding too eager, though. She didn't want him getting suspicious. "Well, I don't know," she said. "I've tentatively agreed to accept a permanent position."

"Oh damn! I was afraid of that." He sounded so anguished that she was ashamed of herself. He was under all the stress he could handle and didn't need her adding to it.

She was about to tell him she'd stay with his daughters when he spoke again. "Look, if I agree to hire you permanently will you come? If you don't mind being the subject of speculation and gossip, I promise you can work for me as long as I need a housekeeper or you need the position. Please, Lark. Whatever salary you've been offered, I'll pay more."

Now she was not only ashamed but hurt. He didn't want her full time, but he'd take her because he couldn't find anyone else. "I'm not blackmailing you, Jonathan. I'll stay with the girls while you're gone, and you won't owe me anything beyond that. I can always get another job." She regretted that the pain she felt had throbbed in her voice.

"I never thought you were blackmailing me." Jonathan said quietly, "and we both know that once you're moved in here I'm not going to ask you to leave. How soon can you come?"

"How soon do you want me?"

"Right now," he said, and hung up.

Lark wondered if he was as aware, as she was, of the dual meanings of those last few sentences.

She explained the situation to Melanie, packed an overnight case and headed for the Nolan home. She could come back later for the clothes and other personal items she'd need.

In her excitement she misread a street sign and took a wrong turn—nothing new for her—but within fifteen minutes she had pulled into the familiar driveway and parked in front of the house. She was just about to ring the bell when the door opened and, without quite knowing how it had happened, she was in Jonathan's arms with her own wrapped tightly around his waist.

He smelled clean, like soap and talcum powder, and his shirt was smooth and crisp beneath her hands. He wasn't wearing anything under it, and her palms explored the taut muscles of his lower back.

They stood silently clinging to each other. There were no fireworks, no searing passion, just the quiet feeling of wholeness, like long-time lovers who communicate beyond passion. Lark could feel his heart beating strong and steady against her breast, and she snuggled deeper into his embrace. He shifted her slightly so that she fitted intimately against him.

After a moment he broke the silence. "Thank you for coming when I needed you," he murmured against her hair.

"Thank you for wanting me," she replied, and nuzzled the side of his neck above his collar.

"Oh, Lark, don't be grateful for that," he groaned. "Wanting you is something over which I have no control, but I don't intend to let it get out of hand. We don't even know each other. As soon as I can I'm going to disentangle myself from you, and from then on we're going to have a strictly employer-employee relationship. Understand?"

"Uh-huh," she said slowly. She did understand. She understood that she couldn't become romantically involved with him as long as she was in his home under false pretenses, but she didn't seem to be able to do anything about it right now. She belonged in his arms, and that's where she wanted to stay.

The spell was finally broken by the dog, Blazer, who came bounding into the house from the back, barking joyously as he skidded around corners to greet his master. Startled, Jonathan and Lark tore themselves apart as the big golden retriever jumped up on Jonathan and licked his face in a frenzy of excitement.

"Down, Blazer," Jonathan ordered as he put out his arms to ward off the animal. "Who let the dog in?" he yelled just before Candace came in from the kitchen.

"Sorry, Dad," she said. "He ran in when I opened the back door."

She spied Lark and her face lit up with a happy smile. "Oh, hi, Lark. Dad says you're going to be our new housekeeper. Great!"

Lark was having trouble coming down to earth, but she managed a weak smile. "Well, I'll be here while your dad's gone. We'll have to see what happens after that."

"No you don't; you can't back out now," Candace teased. "Dad said you were going to stay, so you're committed."

Lark sincerely hoped so.

During the next few days Lark settled in, and she and her charges became better acquainted. They got along fine. She and Candace established an easy rapport, and although

Patty missed her father and cried for him at times, mostly she was content with her sister and Lark as substitutes.

Once Lark and Jonathan had managed to break out of each other's arms the day she came to stay, he had treated her as he'd promised—as a new employee whom he liked and trusted but had little interest in otherwise. He'd given her the only bedroom on the main floor, and when she protested that she might not hear Patty if she should waken in the night, he'd shown her how to work the intercom system between her room and Patty's. "Patty's room is next to mine," he'd explained, "and ordinarily I get up myself if it's necessary. It's only when I'm away from home that you'll be responsible for her at night."

At that, Lark's admiration for this man had increased. How many other men would get up at night with a child when they were paying someone else to care for her?

He was busy the rest of the evening getting ready to leave. The following morning he was to drive to San Francisco International Airport. At bedtime he kissed his daughters goodbye, then gave Lark more last-minute instructions before telling her good night and disappearing into his room. When she awoke the next morning he was gone. He hadn't even said goodbye.

Jonathan called from China on Friday to tell them he had arrived safely and would probably be gone about a week. The call came at noon while Lark was gone from the house to pick up Patty from the day care center, which she was now attending mornings only, so she didn't get to talk to him. Candace relayed the message, and Lark felt an unreasonable stab of disappointment.

By then Lark had met most of the neighbors, thanks to Candace, who introduced her as, "Lark Bancroft, who's going to be staying with us for a while."

Lark could almost see the speculation going on in the neighbors' minds, but she was too pleased by Candace's casual acceptance of her as a friend rather than as an employee to explain. Also, it would make it easier to strike up a conversation with them if she were on the same social level.

Her first opportunity came on Saturday while she was shopping at a nearby supermarket. She was browsing through the produce section when the neighbor in the brick house on the right hailed her. "Hi, Lark," she said, and glanced in the partially filled grocery cart. "Hey, don't tell me you expect those kids of Giselle's—uh—Jonathan's to eat broccoli and brussel sprouts."

Nancy Scottsworth colored slightly with embarrassment at her inadvertent mention of Jonathan's wife. Nancy was a tall slender woman in her late thirties who taught at the college.

Lark was delighted with the slip. It gave her the opening she needed. "Oh dear," she said, "you mean their mother didn't feed them green vegetables?"

Nancy grimaced. "Giselle didn't like vegetables, so she didn't cook them. Her taste ran more to the heavier German-type cooking, dumplings and thick gravy, and cobbler desserts. It was beginning to show on her, too, before she left. Last time I saw her she'd put on at least ten pounds, mostly around the hips."

"When was the last time you saw her?" Lark asked conversationally as she searched for a firm head of lettuce.

"Oh, gee, that would have been the day I testified for Jonathan at the custody hearing last spring. Boy, was she steamed when I got on the witness stand." Nancy paused, then continued. "I can't say I blame her. We'd been friendly for years, but it was for that very reason that I felt I had to take sides. Giselle was a rotten mother."

Lark turned away and pretended an interest in the bunches of celery in order to hide her shock. The Ulrics had insisted their daughter was an exemplary parent, but here was a neighbor, with no family ties to prejudice her, who held a different opinion.

Lark turned back and smiled to take the sting out of her words. "Maybe it just seemed that way to you. Sometimes mothers reach the limit of endurance with their kids and say or do things that outsiders misinterpret."

Nancy was selecting loose potatoes and putting them in a sack on the scale. "Not Giselle. She meant everything she said and did. I felt especially sorry for Candace. She was about eight years old when they built the house next door. A difficult age, I admit, but I never heard Giselle say a kind word to the child. All she ever did was yell and scold and order her around. Then, when Giselle found out she was pregnant again..." Nancy sighed. "Well, I don't have time to stand around gossiping all day. Nice to see you. Stop over later for a drink if you have the time."

She deposited her sack of potatoes in the cart and pushed it ahead of her toward the bakery section, leaving Lark wondering just what had happened when Jonathan's wife discovered she was going to have another baby.

The conversation with Nancy Scottsworth left Lark more puzzled than enlightened. Her observations of Giselle Nolan were the exact opposite of the Ulrics'. Still, each was telling the truth as they saw it. Nancy had no personal involvement, so she was more apt to be objective, but would Alice Ulric allow her devotion to her daughter to blind her if Giselle was mistreating her children? And what about Jonathan? Why hadn't he intervened?

Lark shook her head. No doubt Nancy hadn't meant to imply actual child abuse. She had no children of her own, and her students were college-age adults. Also, she'd been an outside observer, a neighbor who only knew part of what was going on next door. Giselle was probably a high-strung woman whose children got on her nerves. What mother wasn't at times?

Lark was anxious to talk to Harriet Baxter, the neighbor on the left, but she didn't know how to go about it without seeming pushy. The Baxters were in their sixties. He owned a prosperous insurance business and she had always been a homemaker. They'd been most pleasant when Candace introduced Lark to them, but she hadn't seen them since and couldn't think of an excuse to seek them out.

Her problem was solved that same afternoon when Harriet phoned to say she was stirring up a batch of cookies, but that when she'd tried to open the bottle of vanilla it had slipped out of her arthritic fingers and broken. She asked if Lark had some she could borrow.

"Of course," Lark said cheerfully, "I'll bring it right over."

Candace and her friend Maribeth Murphy were in Candace's room listening to her stereo. Lark explained where she was going and asked Candace to listen for Patty, who was napping.

Harriet opened the front door on the first ring of the bell. "Lark, you're a godsend," she said. "Come on in the kitchen and talk to me while I get the first batch ready for the oven."

The Baxters' home was at least as big as Jonathan's, but it was decorated in the more traditional style of the forties. The kitchen was immaculate in spite of the cookie baking in progress.

When Lark was seated at the Formica table with a cup of coffee, Harriet said, "How are you getting along with the Nolan youngsters? You hardly seem old enough to be in charge now that Jonathan is out of the country."

Lark glanced down at the blue jeans and sweatshirt she was wearing, and realized that Candace dressed in the same way. She guessed it was sort of hard to tell the teenagers from the young adults anymore. "I'm twenty-five, Harriet, and I've been married. Although I don't have children of my own, I did a lot of baby-sitting when I was in school. Candace and Patty and I are getting along just fine."

Harriet slid the filled cookie sheet into the oven. "They're sweet children. I adore both of them, but Candace is almost like my own. From the time they moved into the neighborhood when she was about eight, until Patty was born five years later, she spent almost more time here than she did at home. Giselle was gone a lot, and Candace would come here after school and stay till dinnertime. If Jonathan was out of town, which he often was, she'd stay till Giselle came after her. Usually it was very late."

Harriet poured herself a cup of coffee and sat down opposite Lark. "Jonathan and Giselle weren't getting along, even then. Such a shame. They're both nice people. Oh, Giselle was badly spoiled and willful, but you couldn't really blame her. Her parents doted on her and let her do just as she pleased."

She took a sip of her coffee and Lark remained silent, hoping she'd continue without prompting. She did. "Alice Ulric—that's Giselle's mother—and I went to school together. Alice was a pampered only child, and when she married Frederik Ulric he continued to cater to her. I guess it's not surprising that she raised her daughter the same way, but she didn't do Giselle any favor. The child didn't have many girlfriends in school, but the boys flocked around. She was a real beauty, and a born flirt." Harriet sighed. "Poor Jonathan never got to really know her until after they were married, and then it was too late."

Lark understood the situation better now, and a wave of compassion for Jonathan swept over her. How did a caring, thoughtful man like him ever get tied up with such a selfish, unlikable woman as Giselle? Did he love her? He must have; Lark couldn't believe that he'd marry her if he hadn't. If he did, she must have broken his heart. Was he upset enough to frighten her into disappearing?

No. Lark would never believe that. Admittedly she didn't know him very well, but the few hours she'd spent in his company, plus the comments she'd heard from people who'd known him for years, convinced her that he'd never do anything to drive the mother of his children into hiding. Besides, if Giselle was as strong-willed and selfish as people said, then it was unlikely there was anything he could do to make her leave if she didn't want to.

Giselle was a fighter, that much was sure. Twice she'd fought her husband in court for custody of the children she apparently didn't really want. If she'd do that, there wasn't much Jonathan could do or say that would intimidate her. So why did she vanish? Where was she?

Lark knew she had to find out, and the only way to do that was to ask questions just as if she didn't know anything about the subject. She cleared her throat. "Candace never talks about her mother, and so far neither has Jonathan. Does Giselle live around here? I assume Jonathan has custody."

Harriet got up to check the progress of the cookies in the oven. "No, Giselle doesn't live here anymore. At least not that anyone knows of. Jonathan has the children because she disappeared in the middle of a custody hearing a year ago and hasn't been heard from since."

Lark widened her eyes and gasped in assumed surprise. "You mean she just walked away and left her children?"

Harriet carried the baking sheet to the counter and used a spatula to transfer the delicious-smelling chocolate chip cookies to a platter. "Nobody knows," she said. "One day she was in court fighting Jonathan for custody, and the next day she was gone. Just packed her bags and left without a word to anybody, not even her parents or children. The Ulrics demanded a police investigation, but nothing ever came of it. She just closed out her bank account and vanished."

Lark looked convincingly shocked. "But surely Jonathan knows where she is. Wouldn't she keep in touch with him? He must have been paying her support."

Harriet shook her head as she spooned more cookie dough onto the sheet. "No, I'd stake my life on it. The Ulrics are convinced he knows, but he was as shocked and upset as they were when he found out she was gone. He cooperated in every way he could with the police investigation. If he'd heard from her he'd have said so. He's too kind-hearted to do a thing like that."

Lark returned to the Nolan residence a short time later with a container of still-warm cookies and a mind full of conflicting information that was as confusing as it was helpful.

The next day Jonathan again called from China. This time Lark answered the phone, and found that it was actually possible for the heart to leap. Hers did when she heard his voice. "Lark? Is that you? This is Jonathan."

The connection was murky, but by raising their voices and speaking distinctly they could hear. "Yes, this is Lark. How are you, Jonathan?"

"Still suffering from jet lag," he answered. "We had our first meeting two hours after we arrived, and none of us has had a chance to adjust to the time change since."

She could hear the weariness in his tone, and there was a catch in her voice when she answered. "I'm sorry. You do sound tired. Will you be coming home soon?"

"Just as quickly as we can wind things up here. I miss—" he paused for a second before finishing "—my family. How are you and the girls getting along?"

"We're just fine," Lark assured him. "Don't worry about us. I'm sorry Candace isn't here. She went to a movie with some other girls. She'll be upset that she didn't get to talk to you. Patty's asleep, but I can wake her if you—"

"No, don't bother her. Actually, it's you I want to talk to."

A smile of pleasure lit Lark's face, only to be erased by his next words. "Are you sure there are no problems? Do you have enough money? I arranged with the bank to give you more if you need it."

She should have know he wasn't paying for an overseas call just because he wanted to hear her voice, speak with her. He'd called to make sure she was taking proper care of his home and children. She was his housekeeper, not his love.

She was careful to keep the disappointment out of her tone. "Jonathan, please don't worry about us. There are no problems, and you left me with more money than I can possibly spend. I'll take good care of the girls."

"I know you will," he said softly. His tone had become more intimate. "Will you take as good care of me when I get home?"

Before Lark could gather her fragmented thoughts and answer, he growled into the phone, "Oh damn! Forget I said that. I'm tired, and lonely, and not thinking straight. I hope to be home Friday or Saturday. I'll call as soon as I know. Meanwhile, did Candace give you the number where I can be reached here?"

"Yes, she did, but—"

"Don't hesitate to call me. I'm always in my room at this time. It's when I sleep—or try to."

He'd said he was lonely, and it showed through in his voice. She wished she could reach out and take him in her arms, soothe away his depressed mood. If only she could tell him how much she missed him. How eagerly she waited for him to come home.

Instead, she said the only thing she could say. "Jonathan, I'd never call you unless it was a real emergency. It must cost a fortune."

"Sweetheart, money's not my problem." Again his voice became intimate. "I wish you were here with me."

"So do I," she murmured. He'd called her sweetheart! She wondered if he was aware of doing it, or if it was just a casual endearment to him. "Where are you, Jonathan?" She meant what part of China.

He chuckled. "I'm in bed, but that's not exactly what I meant when I said I wish you were with me. If I start thinking about that, I'll never get to sleep. Shall we change the subject? What were you doing when I called?"

Her mind was quicker than her caution, and she pictured him lying in a bed nude except for a sheet that covered him from the hips down. His chest was furred with the dark hair she'd seen peeking from above his partially unbuttoned sport shirt, and the hard muscles that she'd felt when he'd held her rippled as he reached out his arms to her, beckoning her to join him.

She shook her head to dislodge the unwelcome image and hoped her voice wouldn't quiver. "I—I was watching an old movie on television. *Wuthering Heights*, with Laurence Olivier."

"Ah, yes, the story of Heathcliff and Cathy and their undying love." He was being sarcastic. "I'm afraid you're

an incurable romantic, Lark. Surely you know that love i
an illusion fostered by poets and teenage girls.''

Lark was shaken out of her dreamworld. "That's no
true,'' she snapped. ''I know what love is like. I've beer
married, remember?''

"So what's that got to do with it? I've been married, too
and I quickly found out that love is just a poetic euphe-
mism for lust.''

A sudden chill made Lark shiver. Jonathan and Giselle
had been married a long time. Had they been unhappy from
the beginning? How awful for both of them.

"I'm sorry you feel that way,'' she said carefully. ''I loved
my husband when I married him, and I loved him when I
lost him. I guess you could say I still love him, but in a different way. I wish him well. I don't want him to be hurt.''

"If he was such a paragon, why did you divorce him?''
Jonathan sounded angry.

Lark took a deep breath. She'd started this, and she
wasn't going to back down now. ''Because he asked me to,''
she answered. ''He wanted to marry another woman.''

Jonathan grated an obscenity that could have gotten them
disconnected if the overseas operator had heard it. ''Where
in hell's your backbone? I'd never have taken you for one
of those passive turn-the-other-cheek freaks who go through
life asking to be kicked.''

The unexpected attack left Lark gasping. ''Then we were
both wrong,'' she said angrily, not bothering to deny his
unjust accusation. ''Because I'd never have believed you
were so rigid that you'd let one mistake embitter you so.''

"Damn right I'm bitter. That one mistake lasted for fifteen years, and it's not one I'm likely to repeat. Grow up,
Lark, and live in the real world, or you'll be miserable all
your life.''

"But Jonathan, I'm not miserable," she pointed out. "I came to terms with my ex-husband and our divorce long ago, and I've never been happier. You're the one who's hurting."

"Oh for—" She could almost hear the crackle of his exasperation. "Good night, Lark," he barked. "I'll let you know when I'll be home." He slammed the receiver so hard it left a ringing in her ear.

On Monday Lark decided to clean house. She'd picked up the clutter and given it a surface going over the day after she arrived, but now it needed a thorough cleaning. She toyed with the idea of asking Candace to help but then discarded it. She didn't know if the daughter of the house was expected to help the housekeeper with the cleaning, but she decided she'd better let Jonathan mediate that when he got home. That is, if he really intended to let her stay. She did, however, put Candace to work straightening her own room, and got only a mild amount of grumbling.

By late morning she'd worked her way up to Jonathan's room, and while she was dusting the chest of drawers it occurred to her that now was the perfect time to search through his things for evidence of whether he knew what had happened to his ex-wife. She'd instinctively shied away from the distasteful task, but it had to be done and she was the one Rob had hired to do it.

She started by inspecting everything sitting out in full view. The room was decorated in strictly male fashion—heavy functional furniture, tailored bedspread and curtains in shades of brown, rust and green; there was a noticeable absence of the aesthetic adornments a woman would add—figurines, flowers, photographs, and the like. The only wall decoration was an oil painting of a path of sunlight shining through a grove of redwoods. Hardly original, and even to her untrained eye not particularly well executed.

The items in the bathroom were again strictly male—brushes, shaving equipment, a variety of unopened colognes and shaving lotions. Lark smiled. Probably gifts he would never use but couldn't bring himself to throw away.

Back in the bedroom she paused before the closet door. She'd assumed this would be so easy. After all, she was a trained investigator. But she hadn't counted on the human element. She hadn't expected to become emotionally involved with the man she was investigating.

Lark groaned. Emotionally involved! Jonathan was right, she was an incurable romantic. Just because she experienced a few palpitations when he was around didn't mean she was emotionally involved with him. It was a normal reaction for a passionate woman who no longer had an outlet. She'd enjoyed the physical side of her marriage. It had never been a problem. Her difficulty with Wayne had been living with him outside the bedroom.

She gave the doors a shove, and they slid open to reveal a closetful of men's suits, jackets, slacks, shirts and shoes. Nothing to indicate that a woman had ever shared it. She took a deep, shuddering breath and started going through the pockets of his clothes. Dammit, it had to be done. If Jonathan was innocent of the charges the Ulrics had made, then it would do no harm, and if he was guilty he deserved to be exposed. So why did she feel so...disloyal?

Most of the pockets were empty, but she found a gold pen in one jacket and a short black comb and the bill of sale for a doll in another. She figured it was for Varonica Alana, the doll with the red yarn hair and freckles that Patty carried around the house with her so much of the time. As she had been taught, Lark stuck her hand in every shoe and inspected every storage box, but she found nothing.

The chest of drawers proved to be the most difficult. A room, and even a closet, were somewhat impersonal, but her upbringing had taught her that someone else's bureau drawers were off limits. There was something extremely intimate about rummaging through personal items such as underwear, shirts and jewelry. She blushed and hated herself for sneaking around to discover that Jonathan's briefs were the colored bikini type, and that he wore pajamas and preferred the coat-style top.

She rushed to finish, breathing a sigh of relief as she opened the last drawer. It contained an assortment of clothing that was apparently too good to throw out but not in favor for wearing. She hurriedly sorted through the layers and was about to push the drawer shut when her hand contacted something on the bottom that was hard but with a rough nap. As soon as her fingers closed around it she knew it was a picture frame, and she carefully drew it out of the drawer.

It came out facing down, and when she turned it over she saw that it was an eight-by-ten color portrait of a bride and groom in their wedding finery. The man in the tuxedo was Jonathan—a younger, slimmer, more boyish-looking Jonathan, but there was no mistaking his identity, even without the beard.

The girl was radiant in her white satin gown trimmed with seed pearls and lace. Her blond hair was combed up in front to form a setting for the glittering crown that held her long, flowing veil. She carried a bouquet of cascading baby orchids and green fern, and looked small, fragile and breathtakingly beautiful as she snuggled in the arms of her new husband.

A lump formed in Lark's throat and settled in her stomach. The bride's resemblance to Candace Nolan was startling. This was Jonathan and Giselle's wedding portrait.

Jonathan had hidden it away in a drawer, but it was the only photo he kept in his bedroom. Why?

In spite of everything, was Jonathan Nolan still in love with his ex-wife?

Chapter Four

The next morning while Patty was at the day care center and Candace had gone on a picnic with friends, Lark went downtown to see her brother. He was just ushering a distraught young woman out the door when she arrived, and he motioned her into his office.

When he followed a few minutes later, he smiled. "Hi, honey. How's it going? Sit down. I have half an hour before I have to leave for a meeting."

Lark sat on one of the chairs in front of the desk, and Rob settled into the executive chair behind it. "I wish I'd never let you talk me into giving you that assignment," he said cheerfully. "We never see you anymore, and you'll have to return to Phoenix as soon as they assign you to the police academy."

Lark sighed. "I know. I wish I could see more of you and Melanie and the boys, but with Jonathan gone I'm totally tied down. Besides, you and I can't be seen together much. You and Jonathan know too many of the same people."

"When's Jon coming back, do you know?"

"Not for sure. Probably this weekend. In the meantime I've searched the house thoroughly and haven't found a thing to indicate he knows what happened to Giselle or where she is. Honestly, Rob, I think the Ulrics have let their bias against him because of the divorce and custody suit interfere with their good sense."

"I've thought that all along," Rob said, "but they were determined to have him investigated. Have he or the kids said anything about Giselle?"

Lark shook her head. "No, never. Except for a wedding picture I found at the bottom of one of the bureau drawers in his room, there's nothing to indicate that she ever lived there. By the way, do you know where she and the children lived after the marriage broke up?"

Rob thought a minute. "The Ulrics told me that Jon was the one who walked out. He got an apartment, and Giselle and the kids lived in the house. He didn't move in again until after she disappeared."

Lark frowned. "Did he pay spousal support as well as child support?"

"Yes, he did. Giselle claimed that she'd never been trained to earn her own living, and had always been a housewife and mother during their marriage. The judge awarded her a hefty sum every month after she claimed she needed it to keep up her usual standard of living."

"Oh hell!" Lark sputtered. "Where does she get off thinking Jonathan has to support her for the rest of her life? The only thing I got out of my divorce was my freedom and an empty bank account. I didn't even get paid back for all the money I'd spent on Wayne's education. The judge up here must must been either a relative or bribed!"

Rob held up a restraining hand. "Whoa there, sweetie. You know better than that." He grinned. "The poor guy was probably just emotionally seduced. Giselle Nolan is a sexy lady, and she knows how to get what she wants from a man. Any man. No doubt she batted her eyelashes and told him what a helpless little thing she was and reduced him to jelly in the process.

Lark eyed her brother warily. "Did you know her well?"

Rob laughed. "I didn't have to know her well; the whole town knew how she operated. She used her charm on every man she wanted something from. They knew it and they loved it. Oh, I don't mean she went to bed with them," he hastily amended when he saw Lark's shocked expression. "That would have given Jonathan a good excuse to throw her out without the kids *or* the money, and she sure didn't want that. In fact, that's her parents' strongest argument against him now. They claim he not only got custody of his children when she dropped out of sight, but he's saving himself a bundle of money in support payments."

Rob sobered. "They're right, you know. He's a hell of a lot better off without her than he ever was with her."

"Not necessarily," Lark said. "He's pretty bitter." She told Rob of her phone conversation with Jonathan. "I'm afraid he may still be in love with her."

One of Rob's eyebrows rose questioningly. "Afraid? What difference could it make to you if Jonathan Nolan still loves his errant wife?"

"Well, none." Lark was flustered and annoyed with herself. "It's just that he's a nice guy, and I'd hate to see him hurt any more than he has been already. Your Giselle doesn't sound like a very desirable person."

Rob chuckled. "Oh, she's desirable all right," he said with an exaggerated leer, "but she's not *my* Giselle, thank God. I can understand how a man could be all torn up inside over her, though, and I sure hope it hasn't happened to Jon. As you say, he's too nice a guy."

Lark decided she'd better change the subject. She could do without the tender feelings for her employer that this conversation was arousing in her. "Do the Ulrics know you planted me in their son-in-law's house as a housekeeper?"

Rob shook his head. "No, not yet. They left for Alaska before I had a chance to tell them. They probably wouldn't recognize you if they saw you, but I'll contact them as soon as they return and explain the situation."

"Jonathan offered me this job permanently," Lark said, "but in all fairness I feel I should leave as soon as he returns. I don't honestly think there's a chance that I'll turn up any evidence."

Rob's look was speculative. "Does this sort of work bother you, Lark? You're going to have to get used to it if you want to be a police officer."

Yes, it did bother her. More than she liked to admit. She hated sneaking around, going through Jonathan's personal things, gossiping with his neighbors about him. It made her feel . . . sleazy. Jonathan trusted her, and she was betraying that trust. It went against all her moral principles.

She couldn't admit that to her brother, though. He'd pull her off the case and send her back to Phoenix if he so much as suspected that her feelings for the man she was investigating were at all personal. Rob liked Jonathan, but Jonathan was under investigation by Rob's office and that made him off limits for a romantic involvement with Lark or any other employee of that office. It was not only unwise but unethical, and Rob wouldn't stand for it.

Lark couldn't bring herself to look directly at her brother when she answered his question. "No, it doesn't bother me," she lied. "I certainly don't enjoy it, but it's all part of the job. I just—I just don't want the children to get too attached to me when I know I'll be leaving soon. They've already lost their mother."

At least that part was true. She was becoming too fond of Jonathan's daughters, and they of her. There was no way she could get out of this with her own feelings unscathed, but she didn't want to inflict any more pain on Candace and Patty. They were the innocent bystanders who stood to lose the most.

Rob picked up a pencil and tapped it on the desk, a nervous habit of his when he was thinking. "I can understand that, but I want you to observe Jon, and talk to him. So far you haven't even had the opportunity to get acquainted with him."

Lark closed her eyes briefly. Oh, she'd gotten acquainted with Jonathan all right. That had happened the moment his arms clamped around her the second they met. She might not know what he ate for breakfast, or what his favorite television show was, but she knew every muscle in that tall firm body that had pushed so intimately against hers. She knew the way his heart speeded up when he held her, and the sweetness of his warm breath when it brushed her cheek. There was no doubt that she was very well acquainted with Jonathan Nolan!

"I suppose you're right," she agreed reluctantly, not sure if she was sorry or relieved. She wanted to stay on and keep house for Jonathan after he got back home, but she knew that the longer she lived there the more vulnerable she'd become. He had a potent effect on her, one that could lead nowhere. If he ever learned that she'd been investigating him for the Ulrics he'd despise her—and with good reason. Especially if he was as innocent of the charges as he seemed to be. And if he wasn't, she wasn't sure she wanted to know about it.

This was a no-win situation, and the sooner she got out of it the better off she'd be. She suspected that if she delayed much longer it was going to have a profound effect on the rest of her life.

Lark left after assuring Rob she'd continue with the investigation for as long as he needed her, then picked up Patty at the day care center and took her home. It was past noon, and the children had been fed their lunch. Patty nodded sleepily in her car seat as Lark pulled up in the garage.

She gathered the tired little girl in her arms and carried her into the house and up the stairs with the intention of putting her to bed for a nap. The thick carpeting absorbed the footsteps, and the house was quiet as Lark reached the landing and started down the hall toward the nursery.

As she came to the open door of Candace's room she glanced in to see if the girl had made her bed. Lark stopped short. Candace was in the room, but she wasn't alone. There was a young man with her, and they were standing by the draped window wrapped together in an intimate embrace that shocked Lark all the way to her toes.

Good Lord! She hadn't even known Jonathan's daughter had a boyfriend, let alone that they indulged in such passionate kissing. And in the bedroom, yet.

The sharp, involuntary yelp that escaped from Lark's throat wrenched the two lovers apart, their eyes wide with surprise. The surprise turned to horror when they saw Lark standing in the doorway looking equally horrified.

The electrified silence seemed to go on forever until at last Candace spoke. Her voice was pitched high and almost unrecognizable. "Lark! I didn't know you were home!"

"Obviously." Lark's own voice was lower than normal. "Go downstairs, Candace, and wait for me in the den. I'll be down as soon as I put Patty to bed."

She stepped back, but waited until the silent couple had left the room and started downstairs before she continued on to the nursery with the sleeping baby in her arms.

When Lark walked into the pine-paneled den a few minutes later, Candace was standing by the stone fireplace, and the boy was leaning against the desk. In her shocked state Lark hadn't gotten a good look at him before, but now she studied him openly. He was blond, blue-eyed, and almost six feet tall, with the thin, ungainly look common to teenagers who grow too fast for the rest of their bodies to keep up. There was apparently nothing wrong with his hormonal development.

Both he and Candace looked agonizingly embarrassed and frightened. Lark felt a twinge of sympathy. She'd have died if anyone had caught her kissing a boy in such a compromising way when she was sixteen. For the first time, she wondered if she was up to playing substitute mother to a girl only nine years her junior.

She focused her gaze on Candace and spoke. "I think you'd better introduce me to your friend."

The blood had drained from the girl's face, and there were red blotches on her high cheekbones. She glanced at the silent boy. "This is Dirk Olafsson," she said, and her voice trembled. "We go to school together. That is, we did until he graduated this spring."

Lark walked toward the boy and held out her hand. "Hello, Dirk, I'm Lark Bancroft. I'm responsible for Candace and Patty while their father is out of the country."

He took her hand in a quick but firm handshake.

"You don't have to be responsible for me," Candace muttered. "I can take care of myself."

Lark turned toward Candace but ignored the outburst. "Does your father know about Dirk?" she asked.

Candace jutted out her quivering chin. "Of course he
does. We've been dating for months."

Lark decided she might as well get right to the point
"Does he know what else you're doing?"

Both young people gasped and spoke in unison. "We're
not!"

They looked at each other, but this time it was Dirk who
spoke. "Look, we're not doing anything wrong." A blush
stained his white face. "Sure, we make out sometimes, but
we've never, uh, you know," he finished lamely.

"Then why were you in Candace's bedroom?"

Again they both started to speak at once, but it was Dirk
who continued. "That was my fault. She went up there to
get a sweater and I followed her."

Lark felt a spark of admiration for the way he spoke up
to defend Candace, but she wasn't going to let him know
that yet. "You realize, I'm sure, that you were abusing Mr.
Nolan's hospitality."

He looked away. "Well, I—we weren't doing anything.
Just kissing." There was a defensive whine to his tone.

"You forget, I saw what you were doing," Lark snapped,
"and that was no innocent kiss, my friend. It's a good thing
I showed up when I did, and we all three know it. I want you
to leave now, Dirk, and I can't allow Candace to see you
again until her father gets home. He can take over then and
handle it any way he pleases."

Candace gasped. "You're not going to tell Daddy?"

The poor girl looked so terrified that Lark wanted to
reach out to her and assure her that she'd keep her secret.
Instead she made no conciliatory gestures, but her voice
softened as she said, "That's up to you. If you promise not
to see Dirk again until your dad gets home, I'll be selective
in what I report to him, but I'm warning you, Candace, I'm
assuming a lot more responsibility than I should. The

greement will be terminated immediately if you give me
reason to doubt the wisdom of it.''

She knew she came across sounding like a school teacher,
but this was a situation she hadn't counted on and she was
upset and embarrassed.

Candace was less than appreciative. ''But Dirk's been
gone for *two weeks*!'' she cried. ''He just got back in town
this morning, and we were going to a rock concert tonight.
We almost never get rock groups to come to this dumb city,
it's too small. Please, Lark, I'll come right home afterward, I swear.''

Lark knew only too well how long a two-week separation
could be when you were in the throes of teenage infatuation, and she was not unsympathetic, but she stood her
ground. ''I'm sorry, but the answer is no. If you prefer, I can
call your father, explain the problem to him, and ask how
he wants it handled.''

''No,'' Candace screeched. ''He'd ground me for a year!''

The girl realized immediately that she'd given away too
much, and clamped her hand over her mouth. ''Oh, all
right,'' she stormed. ''You're just being hateful, but if that's
the way you want it...'' She didn't continue, but reached out
a hand to Dirk, who took it. ''Are you going to let me tell
him goodbye?''

Lark suppressed a smile at her injured tone. ''Of course,
but do it in the entryway.''

She turned toward the kitchen, wondering if she was
doing the right thing. Had she overreacted? No, she didn't
think so. Teenagers' emotions could be urgent and compel-
ling, and their control wasn't always reliable. Dirk was at an
age when he wanted more than kissing and hand holding,
and Candace was a sweet, vulnerable young lady who might
let him pressure her into giving more than she was ready for.
She needed to be protected from herself.

Lark heard the front door open and close, and a few seconds later the door to Candace's room slammed shut with a defiant bang.

For the next two days Candace was sulky and uncommunicative. She spoke when spoken to, and did what few chores and baby-sitting Lark asked her to, but she spent a lot of time in her room. Candace was well liked by everybody, but by her own choice she was something of a loner. Maribeth Murphy was her only close friend, and Dirk was apparently the only boy she went out with on a regular basis. She was invited to parties and took part in the activities that her social group were involved in, but usually she preferred one or two friends at a time rather than a gang.

Until now, though, she had been a happy, friendly girl content with the low-key life she had chosen. That's why it was so upsetting to Lark to see her turn inward and refuse to share her anger and pain. If she would only yell, argue, throw things, Lark could have handled it, but her silence was devastating. The people with explosive personalities had an outlet for their rage. It was the quiet ones who kept it all bottled up until it festered and caused problems.

That's why Lark readily agreed when Maribeth's mother phoned on Thursday morning to ask if Candace could spend the day with her and her daughter. She explained that they were going to the private racket club for tennis and lunch, and then she added casually, "This is women's day at the club, and I'll be with the girls all the time."

"Thank you," Lark said, and meant it. "I gather you know about our...problem over here?" Mrs. Murphy sounded young and concerned, and Lark needed some moral support.

"Only that you've forbidden Candace to see Dirk until her father gets back." She chuckled. "Maribeth assures me that Candace is totally innocent of any wrongdoing, which teen language means it was something fairly serious that made you take such measures.''

Lark sighed. "It was. Or at least *I* thought it was, and I prefer for her father to handle it."

"Wise girl," the other woman said. "We'll pick Candace up in about half an hour, and bring her home around four. Would you mind if I stayed a few minutes at that time for coffee and a chat?"

"Please do. I've been hoping to meet you." Lark felt relieved, and hoped this lady was as nice as she sounded on the phone.

Iris Murphy was everything Lark had hoped she would be—under forty, understanding and sympathetic. She was also lovely to look at with her red-gold hair, blue eyes, and trim figure.

Candace was actually giggling when they returned that afternoon, but she sobered when she saw Lark and led Maribeth upstairs to her room. Lark invited Iris into the living room where she had coffee and freshly baked peanut butter cookies set out on the coffee table. "I put cookies and milk in Candace's room for the girls," she told Iris as they sat together on the sofa. "I knew that was the first place Candace would head for. She's spent a lot of time up there the past couple of days."

Iris's gaze roamed over Lark in a friendly perusal. "For one so young, you're showing a lot of good sense in handling teenagers. I'd expected you to be older."

"Yes, my age is a problem," Lark answered. "I probably won't be staying long once Jonathan comes home. He thinks I'm too young to live here with him."

Iris raised one delicate eyebrow. "He's right, you know. Jonathan doesn't need that kind of temptation. Pity, though. Up until a few days ago Candace has been bubbling over with praise for you, and I'm impressed that you had the guts to take an unpopular stand with her. Do you want to tell me what happened? I'm almost one of the family. Jonathan, Giselle and I all went to school together, and we've been best friends all our lives.''

Lark hesitated. She hadn't intended to discuss Candace's indiscretion with anyone except possibly Jonathan, but if Iris was a close family friend maybe she could help. Lark needed advice on whether or not to tell Jonathan about his daughter's actions. "It—it's not so much what Candace and Dirk were doing that concerns me as what it could lead to.''

She told Iris of the incident and the circumstances surrounding it. "They weren't doing anything really wrong,'' she concluded. "They were standing up and fully clothed. If I'd found them in the kitchen, or even the living room, I wouldn't have been so upset, but Candace's bedroom—'' She gestured uncertainly. "That young man intended to seduce her if he could, and Candace is so young...''

Iris frowned. "You did exactly what I would have done, Lark. Dirk's no better or worse than any other eighteen-year-old male, but Candace is still too naive to play that sort of game. So is Maribeth, and we keep a close watch on her. Are you going to tell Jonathan?''

Lark sighed. "I don't know. He has a right to know, but I can understand how Candace feels. It wasn't all that long ago that I was her age. The problem is that I don't know Jonathan well enough to gauge how he'd react. If only the poor child had a mother...''

Iris grimaced. "She's probably better off without Giselle. She'd no doubt have ignored the situation and hoped it would go away. She was never one to face up to unpleasantness—unless of course she was the one involved. Giselle and I were very close, but that doesn't mean I was blind to her faults.''

Lark knew she'd have to question this woman about her friend, and it might as well be now even though she hated the idea. "Do you know where Mrs. Nolan is, Iris?"

"No," Iris said emphatically. "I know that both the Ulrics and Jonathan suspect that I've heard from her, but I haven't. It's true we always confided in one another, and I'm certain that if Giselle had contacted anybody it would have been me, but she hasn't. This isn't the first time she's disappeared, you know."

"No, I didn't." Lark's eyes were wide with surprise. "What happened the other time?"

"*Times*, actually. There were two of them."

Good heavens! If this was true, why hadn't someone else mentioned it? Surely the Ulrics must have known. Why didn't they say something? It certainly put a different light on the whole thing.

Iris continued speaking. "The first was when she was about Candace's age. Her parents were far too permissive—neither of them could say no to her—but this time she wanted to spend the weekend in San Francisco with a group of older college kids, both male and female. No chaperons, of course, and it was known that most of them smoked pot."

Iris grinned in remembrance. "Her father finally put his foot down, said absolutely not, and no amount of tears or pleading would persuade him. Giselle was furious. Not so much because she wanted to go with the group but because Frederik had dared to refuse her something she'd asked for. When she saw that he wasn't going to give in, she got in her car and drove off. She was gone for two days, during which her parents were in a state of panic. When she came back there was no more opposition. They never said no to her again."

Lark slumped back on the sofa. "How sad," she said quietly. "Didn't they realize what a disservice they were doing to their daughter?"

Iris shrugged. "I doubt it. But Giselle met her match when she tried the same thing with Jonathan years later."

So Jonathan had been through this before. Lark felt unaccountably depressed. He must have loved his willful wife very much to have stayed with her for so many years. Why were nice guys like him attracted to women who were destined to put them through purgatory?

"What happened that time?" she asked.

Iris rummaged in her purse and drew out a gold cigarette case. "Do you mind if I smoke?"

"No, go right ahead," Lark replied, and watched the other woman light a cigarette with a lighter that matched the case.

Iris inhaled, then blew out a puff of smoke as she settled back. "Jonathan wasn't inclined to take much of Giselle's nonsense, and he did a pretty good job of keeping her in line, but she resented it. They had some real rows, and once when Candace was about five Giselle wanted something—I don't even remember what it was now—that Jonathan wouldn't let her have, and she pulled her little disappearing act again."

Iris took another deep draw on her cigarette. "Instead of being worried, Jonathan was furious. She was gone three days, and when she came back he told her that if she ever did that again he'd leave her and take Candace with him." Iris laughed. "It scared the hell out of Giselle. She had good reason to know that he never made idle threats, and she didn't want to lose him. In her own selfish way she really loved that man."

Jonathan Nolan stepped out of the shower and wrapped a towel around his waist. He'd been sleeping in the nude since he'd been in China. He'd always preferred going to bed that way, but once he'd become the only adult with two daughters in the house he'd found it more expedient to wear pajamas. He never knew when the girls would barge into his room, or when he'd have to get up in the night with Patty.

He slid his gold watch back onto his wrist. Ten minutes past midnight. God but he was tired. His system still hadn't caught up with the time change, and now he'd be going through the same thing again backward. It wouldn't be so bad if he could sleep on the plane, but even when traveling first class he couldn't get comfortable enough in the seat to relax and snooze.

He sat down on the side of the bed and reached for the phone. It was Friday in California, and he hadn't talked to Lark since Sunday. He'd kept hoping she'd want to talk to him badly enough to call him, but she hadn't.

He placed the call with the overseas operator, then moved onto the upholstered chair to wait for it to go through. He wondered if Lark would be as happy to have him back as he would be to be home.

He rubbed his eyes with his fingertips. Damn, he was going to have to stop thinking about her like that. She was just his housekeeper, nothing more. There was no reason why she should care where he was, as long as she had enough money to run the household.

He leaned back and closed his eyes, and immediately a picture of her formed in his mind: her hair, light brown with golden highlights and just enough loose curl to give it body, swirling around her slender shoulders: her expressive almond-shaped green eyes, with thick lashes that were long and several shades darker than her hair; her generous mouth, the lips full and ripe for kissing; her breasts, just about the right size to fit nicely into his cupped hands; and those hips that swayed when she walked and swirled her skirt around her shapely calves.

He muttered a sharp oath and opened his eyes. Why Lark? He'd dated a lot of attractive women since his divorce, taken some of them to bed, but never had one of them haunted him the way Lark Bancroft was doing. He didn't even know her. Had only held her in his arms once, unless you counted the time he was comforting her when her hand was slammed in the door. Hell, he'd never even kissed her!

What was the matter with him anyway? Why did he think of her during the day and dream of her at night? Maybe he just needed a woman. It had been quite a while. Those things were difficult to arrange now that he had his girls with him. He didn't like to stay out late, and he wasn't about to take a woman home to share his bed. Being a single father was a whole different ball game from being a swinging bachelor. Besides, he had thought he'd gotten used to the celibate state after those last few years of his disastrous marriage.

The ring of the telephone interrupted his uncomfortable thoughts, and he hurried across the room to answer it. It was the overseas operator, and in a few seconds he heard Lark's lilting voice. "Jonathan, I was hoping you'd call soon."

She sounded happy to hear from him, and the thought lightened his mood. "Hello, honey. I've been waiting all week for you to call me."

"But I didn't have any reason to call," she said, sounding puzzled.

Didn't she know that as far as he was concerned, just hearing her voice was reason enough for her to call. No, of course she didn't, and he wasn't about to tell her. He was just homesick, lonesome, and this stupidity would pass once he was back again with his family.

Instead he said, "How's everything on the home front? Are the girls giving you any trouble?"

It seemed to him that she hesitated just a fraction too long before she replied, "Everything's fine. Do you know yet when you'll be back?"

"That's one of the reasons I'm calling. I'll be arriving in San Francisco Sunday morning, and should be home by dinnertime that evening."

"Oh, golly, that's great." He was sure he could hear a smile in her voice. "The girls will be so happy to see you."

"Will you be happy to see me, too?" he asked, and could have bitten his tongue.

Her voice deepened. "Yes, I'll be happy to see you, too."

The warmth in her tone produced a corresponding warmth in him, and he was suddenly aware that he was nude except for the towel. "I've missed you, Lark," he said softly, and regretted the huskiness of his voice.

For a moment neither of them spoke; then Lark cleared her throat rather self-consciously and asked, "Did you ever catch up on your rest?"

He smiled, pleased with her concern. "Not really. I intend to sleep for days once I get back to Eureka." He had to clamp his jaws together to keep from asking if she'd curl up in his arms and sleep for days with him.

If he didn't bring this conversation to a close soon he was going to say something he'd regret later. "Look, I'd better hang up and try to get some sleep. We have another meeting scheduled tomorrow before we leave, and then it's a twelve-hour flight from Beijing to San Francisco. I'll take you all out to dinner Sunday evening."

Again Lark hesitated. "If you don't mind, I'd rather cook dinner here. You'll be exhausted by the time you drive all the way from San Francisco.'' Again her warmth seemed to radiate over the lines.

"I'd like that, Lark," he murmured. "Thank you."

It wasn't until after he'd broken the connection that he remembered he hadn't even asked to speak to his daughters.

Chapter Five

By Sunday afternoon Lark had the house sparkling clean and dinner in the oven. The smell of roasting beef wafted from the kitchen, the salad greens were torn and stored in an airtight container in the refrigerator, and she'd just finished frosting the chocolate cake. The table in the dining room was set with the good china and silver, and even Candace was in a happy mood for a change.

It wasn't until Lark started assembling the ingredients for the salad dressing that she realized she'd forgotten to buy Roquefort cheese and would have to go to the grocery store. She could send Candace, but Jonathan had told her he didn't want his daughter driving while he was gone and had taken all the car keys with him. Candace had never driven Lark's car, and since the old Mustang was temperamental, Lark didn't want to send her off in it alone.

She checked the time. Four o'clock. Patty was still napping, but Candace could stay with her while Lark was gone. She ran upstairs and explained the situation to Candace, who in honor of her father's homecoming was changing into a new pair of designer jeans and a long bulky rose-colored sweatshirt with a tick-tack-toe design. Lark was already dressed in a lilac silk jersey dress that hugged her high breasts and small waist, then swirled nicely around her nylon-clad legs.

Candace agreed to listen for Patty in case she should waken, and Lark left for the market. There was a small convenience store in the neighborhood, but they didn't carry gourmet items like fresh Roquefort cheese, so she had to drive several miles to find a specialty store open on Sunday. While there she picked up a few other items she knew she'd need in the next day or two, and the proprietor seemed bored and prone to chat, so it was several more minutes before Lark broke away.

As she neared the Nolan home she glanced at the clock on the dash and found that she'd been gone almost forty-five minutes. She hadn't realized it would take her so long. She swung into the curved driveway and parked behind a long black Lincoln Continental. Jonathan's car. He was home!

She grabbed the bag of groceries and hurried up the walk, her heart racing with excitement and anticipation. She'd been feeling like a moonstruck schoolgirl ever since he'd told her he was coming home. Now, finally, he was here.

As soon as she unlocked the door and opened it she heard Patty crying. She must have woken up when her father came in.

Lark followed the sound to the living room and found Jonathan pacing the floor trying to soothe the sobbing child in his arms. A big smile split Lark's beaming face as she walked toward them. "Jonathan. Welcome home."

The man who swung around to face her was a stranger. He had Jonathan Nolan's features, but that was where the resemblance ended. His face was white, his jaws clenched, is eyes shuttered, and the look he turned on her was one of pure out-of-control rage. "Where in hell have you been?" he shouted above Patty's screams. "And why did you leave my baby daughter alone in this house while you were gone for God knows how long?"

Lark was too shocked to speak coherently. "I—I didn't..."

"Don't lie to me, dammit!" He cuddled the crying child closer and massaged her back lovingly. "I heard Patty screaming even before I got in the house, and when I ran upstairs I found her caught half-in and half-out of her crib, all alone and absolutely terrified!"

Lark reeled from the stunning impact of his words, and from the fury with which he hurled them at her. "But—but Candace is here—"

She broke off, unable to continue. Obviously Candace was *not* here, but where was she? Candace knew Lark had left her in charge of her little sister. She'd agreed to it. It wasn't like Candace to take off and leave the baby in the house alone.

Jonathan's mouth twisted in disgust. "Candace is not here, and hasn't been since I got home half an hour ago. So help me, Lark, you'll pay for this. I'm going to have you charged with criminal child neglect. There's no telling what might have happened to Patty if I hadn't come home when I did. Just how often have you left her alone while I've been gone?"

He was positively livid, and Lark stumbled back, dropping the sack of groceries on a table without even being aware of it. She was trembling so that she could hardly stand, and when her leg bumped against a chair she sank down into it. "I only went to the store." Her words were almost unintelligible, even to her own ears. "Patty was asleep,

but Candace knew I was leaving. She was here. She agree
to stay until I got back.''

"Don't try to put the blame on Candace," he snarle
"She'd never leave her sister alone. I should have my min
examined for trusting you with my children."

Patty, apparently frightened by the intensity of her fa
ther's anger, wailed lustily, and Jonathan turned away fro
Lark and murmured comforting words in an effort to rea:
sure her and get her to stop crying.

Lark was too stunned to move as she sat staring afte
them. She'd walked into the middle of a nightmare! Sh
couldn't blame Jonathan for being upset. What paren
wouldn't be under the circumstances? Just the thought o
poor little Patty being caught half-in and half-out of her cri
and no one responding to her terrified screams made Lar
ill, but why wouldn't he at least listen to her explanation
And where was Candace? Had something happened to he
too?

Lark was so upset that her teeth chattered, and she wasn
at all sure her rubbery legs would hold her, but she pushe
herself up out of the chair and started toward Jonathan
Just then the back door slammed and she heard footstep
crossing the kitchen tile. A moment later Candace walke
into the living room. She was wearing her miniature radi
clipped to her belt with the headphones fitted snugly agains
her ears.

There was no outward sound from the radio, but Lar
knew that Candace could hear nothing but the rock musi
that was blasting in her ears at a deafening pitch.

Jonathan stopped dead still, and Lark sank back down i
the chair as her legs gave way. Candace's innocent face lit u
with pleasure when she saw her father, and she switched of
the radio. "Dad, you're home," she squealed as she pulle

ff the headphones and tossed them and the radio into a
earby chair.

She started across the room toward Jonathan, then
opped when she saw the look of utter disbelief on his white
ace. She turned her head to look at Lark. "Lark, what are
ou doing back so soon?" Then as if just realizing that
atty was crying and clinging to their father, she said,
'What's the matter with Patty? I didn't hear her crying."

Jonathan finally found his voice. "Where did you come
rom?"

"I've been out in back," she said. "Sitting on the bluff
nd listening to my radio."

Lark knew the bluff. It was outside the fence that en-
losed their backyard, and could only be reached by a gate
hat was kept locked. The gate was about one hundred feet
rom the back of the house. If Candace had been on the
luff with her radio turned up high, there was no way she
ould possibly have heard the commotion going on in the
ouse.

"How long have you been there?" Jonathan demanded,
nd Lark could detect the anger returning to his tone.

"Only since Lark left to go to the store. It's been
bout..." She looked at her watch and gasped. "Oh my
osh, it's been almost an hour!"

"And during that time you were supposed to be listening
or Patty to wake up?" His anger was building rapidly.

Candace blanched as she finally realized that she was in
eep trouble. "Yes, but I was right here... Oh no! Did
omething happen to her? I didn't hear anything."

"Of course you didn't!" Jonathan's rage returned full
orce. "How could you with that radio blaring in your ears?
Your little sister could have been killed here all by herself,
nd you'd never have heard it."

He was shouting at Candace now the way he had earli[er] at Lark, and Lark couldn't stand it any longer. This wa[s] between Jonathan and his daughter, and all she could thin[k] of was escape, putting distance between her and this who[le] awful scene.

She stood and made her way to the kitchen on her trem[bling] legs, then out the back door and across the patio. Sh[e] could still hear Jonathan's raised voice, and she continue[d] on across the wide expanse of lawn and flower garden[s]. Candace's refuge beckoned, and she unhooked the gat[e] then hooked it again behind her and stood on the wide ledg[e] where the bluff extended out before tapering down to th[e] water of the bay.

She cursed the high heels of her sandals as she stumble[d] down the slope until she reached another, narrower ledg[e] partially hidden by gnarled old pine trees. She slumpe[d] down onto the needle-covered ground and drew her legs u[p] against her chest, wrapping her arms around her shins an[d] burying her face in her knees. Her body still shook, an[d] tears that were dammed up behind her eyes fought to burs[t] free, a luxury she refused to allow.

She wasn't going to cry. She wouldn't let Jonathan No[-] lan make her cry. He'd been cruel and unreasonable, but sh[e] was trained as a police officer. She'd been taught how t[o] handle this sort of personal attack by distraught men an[d] women, how to diffuse their anger and help them get it u[n-] der control.

So why *didn't* she, dammit? Why had she run away to s[it] here like a mound of quivering jelly? Why did Jonatha[n] Nolan have the power to flay her with his unjust accusa[-] tions? He had, after all, come home from a long absence t[o] find his small daughter in danger and screaming with te[r-] ror, and no one available to protect her. He'd reacted as an[y] caring parent would have. He'd found the person he'd lef[t]

n charge and raised hell. She'd have done the same thing if
their positions had been reversed, so why was she taking it
so personally?

She took a deep breath and made a concentrated effort to
relax. There was no way to salvage this mess. She never
should have gotten involved in the first place. Rob had been
right, she was too inexperienced both with investigations
and with men. She never should have let herself fall in love
with Jonathan.

Fall in love! Lark clamped her palms over her ears as if
covering them would shut out the voice of her thoughts. She
couldn't be in love with Jonathan; she hadn't known him
long enough. Besides, she wasn't stupid enough to become
emotionally involved with a man she was investigating.

Oh, wasn't she? She'd been emotionally involved with
him before she'd ever taken on the case. Before she'd even
known who he was. Her body had reacted to his arms
around her even while her bruised hand was shooting pain
all the way to her shoulder. She was a congenital idiot! She
should have turned and run as fast as she could when she
first discovered that he was the man she'd come to spy on.

He was right, but for the wrong reasons. He shouldn't
have trusted her. Her primary reason for being in his home
wasn't to care for his children, but to sneak, and pry, and
gossip. To snoop into the most private areas of his life, his
relationship with his wife. He blamed Lark for something
she hadn't done, but what she had done to him without his
knowledge was even more unforgivable.

Once again tears threatened to spill over, but she took a
deep breath and hung on doggedly. The only thing she could
do now was get out as gracefully as possible and hope that
her heart wasn't totally involved. Jonathan probably
wouldn't carry out his threat to have her charged with child
endangerment now that Candace had backed up her story.

If it was agreeable to him, she'd finish and serve dinner, the pack and leave as quickly as she could. It was almost a re lief to be done with the whole unsavory business. She' never again work as a private investigator, and for the firs time she was having second thoughts about her qualifica tions as a police officer.

She raised her head and gazed out at the churning sea. Sh would miss the ocean, but she'd spent all her life in the de sert and now it was time to go back to Phoenix. She'd spen tomorrow with Rob and Melanie, and then leave the fo lowing day for home. If she left now, Jonathan would neve have to know who she really was, or her true reason fo seeking the position as his housekeeper.

After a while she rose, dusted off the back of her dres and returned to the house. All was quiet, the main floo apparently deserted.

She went into the kitchen and took the meat, potatoes an carrots, which she'd been cooking all together in a bakin bag, out of the oven and set them on the stove top. Sh found the sack of groceries in the living room where she' dropped them, and made the fateful salad dressing that ha been the cause of the explosion.

Where were Jonathan and the girls? She hadn't heard sound since coming into the house, but a quick look out th window confirmed that Jonathan's car was still parked ou front. They must be upstairs. She'd better go up and le them know that dinner would be ready in a few minutes.

She walked to the bottom of the stairs, then stopped an took a deep breath. What was she going to find when she go up there? She wished she could just leave and not need t confront any of them again, but she couldn't do that. Sh had to be sure everything was all right between Candace an her father.

She climbed the stairs and started down the hall, but when she came to Candace's room the sound of deep sobs stopped her. Without considering the right or wrong of her actions, she opened the door and went in. Candace was flung full length on the bed, her face buried in a pillow, sobbing wretchedly.

Lark hurried across the room and sat down on the side of the bed. She put her hand on the girl's heaving shoulder and murmured, "Candace, darling, don't cry so. You'll make yourself sick."

Candace turned her head and looked up, then scrambled to a sitting position and threw herself into Lark's arms. "Oh, Lark," she moaned, "it was awful. Daddy's never yelled at me that way before. I honestly think he would have taken me across his knee and spanked me if he hadn't had Patty in his arms. I've never seen him so mad." She dissolved in a flood of tears as Lark held her close.

Lark felt a sickening wave of guilt. She should have stayed and tried to deflect some of Jonathan's rage from the child, but she'd been afraid of making it worse. He wouldn't have welcomed her interference. Besides, she'd been as shocked as his daughter was now, and in no condition to defend anyone. Not even herself.

She gently stroked Candace's shoulders and back, trying to calm her. "It'll be all right, honey. It's really me he's angry with. He thought I'd gone away and left Patty all alone in the house. He was just in the middle of chewing me out when you came in."

Candace raised her tear-stained face. "You mean he yelled at you, too?"

Lark managed a faint smile. "I think 'roared' would be a better way of putting it. Try to see your father's side of it, Candace," she said, growing more serious. "I'm sure he told you what he found when he got home. He had good

reason to be upset with both of us. I should have waite
until Patty woke up and taken her to the store with me, bu
since I left you in charge instead, you should have staye
right here in the house, without the radio and earphones."

Candace nodded. "I know. I won't make that mistak
again. Dad smashed the earphones and took the radio awa
from me. He also grounded me for two weeks, and he say
I can't drive the car for the rest of the summer." A new so
tore through her, and she again buried her face in Lark'
shoulder.

"I'm sorry," Lark said, brushing the damp mahogan
hair back from the girl's wet cheek, "but what you did wa
not only thoughtless but dangerous. You deserve to be dis
ciplined, but maybe he'll relent a little once he's had time t
think it over calmly. Meanwhile, dinner will be ready in te
minutes, so you'd better go wash your face. By the way
where's Patty?"

Candace straightened and wiped her streaming cheek
with the palms of her hands. "Dad took her to his bed
room. He said something about taking a shower."

Lark stood and looked down at her grieving charge. "Jus
remember, my dear, that he loves you very much. He
wouldn't get so upset when these things happen if he didn't
so try to make allowances for the fact that he's human jus
like everyone else's father, and sometimes he overreacts."

Candace lowered her gaze to the bed. "I know. Lark, I'm
glad you're here. I—I'm sorry I've been such a brat this
week." She looked up again, startled. "Oh gee, you aren'
going to tell Dad about *that*, are you?"

In all the confusion, Lark had forgotten about the episode between Candace and Dirk. Now she shook her head
and smiled. "No, I won't tell him, but I want your promise
that you'll be more—restrained—with Dirk in the future."

"Oh, I will," Candace hastened to assure her, "but I wouldn't have done anything wrong that day, honest."

Lark started walking toward the door. "Maybe not," she said, "but don't put it to the test in the future." She opened the door. "Remember, ten minutes. I think the roast is already overcooked."

Lark had just started on down the hall toward Jonathan's room when the door opened and he came out with Patty in his arms. She was quiet now, and obviously he had washed her face and brushed her hair, but she was sucking on her two fingers and huddled close against him.

Jonathan looked ghastly. They both stopped when they saw each other, and for the first time she realized that she'd been too shocked and upset to really observe him before. His face was still bloodless, and his eyes were filled with an indefinable torment. There were deep lines at the corners that hadn't been there before he left the country, and the blue-black shadows underneath were mute evidence of the sleeplessness he had mentioned during their phone conversations. His mouth was set in a taut line, and a pulse pounded beneath his jaw. His shoulders slumped, and his stance was that of a man on the raw edge of total exhaustion.

Their gazes caught and held, and for a moment neither of them said anything. Lark wanted to put her arms around him and help shoulder some of his burdens, but how could she when she was one of them?

Jonathan spoke first. "Thank you for coming back," he said quietly. "Have you seen Candace?"

He must still be angry with her. She'd hoped... "She's in her room," Lark said, trying to keep the disappointment out of her tone. "I've just come from her. Dinner will be ready in ten minutes."

"I have to talk to her," he said. "I'm afraid I was—overly harsh. Can you give us fifteen minutes?"

Lark felt a wave of relief. He was going to apologize to his daughter. If only he could extend his forgiveness to include her, too. "Take as much time as you need," she said softly. "Do you want me to take Patty?"

She held out her arms to the child, but Patty shied away from her and hid her head in her father's shoulder. Jonathan's arms tightened around her, and he shook his head. "No, I'll keep her with me." He walked past Lark to knock on Candace's door.

Lark hurried downstairs, stung by the rejection she'd received from both father and daughter. Obviously Jonathan no longer trusted her with his children. Again she fought back tears.

The meal Lark had worked so hard to prepare was a strain on everybody. The painful tension was thick, and efforts to reduce it were met with polite attempts at conversation that fell flat and only made things worse. Jonathan discussed his trip to China briefly, and a subdued Candace gave him a quick rundown on activities here at home. She didn't mention Dirk at all.

Lark sat quietly, speaking only when spoken to and pushing her overcooked food around her plate. She forced down one bite of the salad, then pushed it away and wondered if she'd ever again be able to eat Roquefort cheese.

Afterward, Jonathan took Patty upstairs to give her a bath and put her to bed. As far as Lark knew he'd been carrying the child around in his arms or had her at his side ever since he'd gotten home. She could understand his concern, but catering to Patty's dependency would only make matters worse. If he didn't start assuring her that this frightening experience was only an unpleasant episode, to be accepted and then forgotten, she would quickly discover she could use it as a means of gaining her beloved daddy's exclusive attention.

Jonathan hadn't asked for her advice, however, and she knew it would be unwelcome if she tried to force it on him. The sooner she got out of there the better.

It was after nine o'clock when she finished cleaning up the kitchen, and she ached with fatigue, not so much physical as emotional. The past few hours had been shockingly intense, and they were taking their toll on everyone. She hadn't seen Jonathan since he'd taken Patty upstairs, and she wondered if he'd gone to bed too. He'd looked so utterly weary.

Still, she couldn't leave the house without telling him she was going. Although he was home, he was in no condition to be responsible for anything tonight. He needed sleep desperately. In the past week he'd made two trips across the Pacific ocean with the resulting jet lag, had spent long days in meetings and then had difficulty sleeping in a strange bed in a foreign land, and today, after twelve hours in the air, he'd driven almost three hundred miles from San Francisco to Eureka. When he finally arrived home he'd had the appalling experience of finding his little daughter endangered, terrified and alone in the house. It's no wonder he was nearly out on his feet.

Lark found Candace in the living room watching television. In answer to her question, Candace said her father was on the phone in the den. Rather than interrupt him, Lark decided to go to her room and pack, but when she walked out of the living room she saw him at the foot of the stairs. He was probably going to his room, she thought, so she had to speak up now.

"Jonathan," she called, and he stopped with one foot on the bottom step and his back to her. "I'm going to leave now, just as soon as I can get my things together." Her lower lip trembled, and she touched it with her finger to steady it. "I can't tell you how very sorry I am that I abused your trust in me. I—"

Jonathan stumbled and threw his hand out to steady himself.

Lark was beside him almost before his hand hit the wall, and then she was in his arms. He leaned heavily against the wall for support and pulled her to him. She wrapped her own arms around his waist in a sustaining embrace. "Darling, are you all right?"

He rubbed his bearded cheek in the soft fragrance of her hair, but he didn't speak. She melted against him and buried her face in his shoulder. For several moments they stood there, propped against the wall and holding each other. Lark could feel him slowly begin to relax, and she wasn't sure whether he was clutching her so tightly because he wanted her in his arms, or if he needed her to hold him up. Either way he needed her, and for now that was enough.

Finally she realized that she'd have to get him upstairs before he collapsed, and she murmured, "I think I'd better put you to bed."

For a minute he continued to hold her; then he straightened up, pulling them away from the wall, and with one arm still around her waist he started climbing the stairs. She kept one of her arms around his waist to support him as they moved.

They continued on to his room, where she turned on the light and led him to the bed. He tumbled onto it and stretched out with a tired sigh. She removed his shoes, then started unbuttoning his shirt, but he captured her hand in his. "No, don't," he said. "I can undress myself."

She felt the accursed blush that was becoming much too familiar, and looked away from him. "I—I wasn't going to undress you, just make you more comfortable."

She tried to rise, but he grabbed her by the wrists and kept her beside him on the bed. "Please don't go away, Lark." His voice held a note of pleading.

"All right," she said. "I'll stay tonight and until you wake up tomorrow. Now get some sleep. I won't leave the house. I promise I'll take good care of the girls."

"I know," he said on a sigh, and his grip on her hands relaxed. He was asleep.

She got a blanket from the linen closet and covered him, then stroked a lock of dark hair off his forehead and leaned over to brush her lips across his. She knew he was too deeply asleep to notice, and tomorrow he would send her on her way with a frosty goodbye.

A sob escaped her throat, but she quickly smothered it. She wasn't going to cry over Jonathan Nolan. She should have known better than to get involved with him in the first place.

By midnight Lark had seen Candace settled in her bed, checked on Patty, who slept peacefully in her crib, and soaked in a tub filled with steamy water and bubbles in the hope of relaxing enough so she could sleep. But she knew it was a vain hope, and after slipping into a cream satin nightgown with spaghetti straps and a low-cut bodice, she selected an anthology of short stories from the bookcase headboard, turned off the overhead light and crawled into bed.

She reached up and turned on the bed lamp, then adjusted her pillows against the headboard and leaned back. Maybe if she read for a while she'd drop off to sleep.

She settled herself comfortably and turned to the first story, but the print blurred and her mind refused to focus on anything but the dreadful scene with Jonathan. How had everything gotten out of hand so quickly, and so violently? When she'd left the house that afternoon everything had been quiet, serene and under control. Less than an hour later she'd returned to chaos and rage. Had she been wrong to leave Candace in charge of the baby for a short time?

No. She knew she hadn't. Since their last housekeeper had left more than a month before, Candace had had full charge of Patty during the hours Jonathan was away from home. There had been no reason for Lark not to trust her, and Jonathan must realize that now. Still he hadn't attempted to apologize, and she knew better than to read anything into the moment of weakness when he'd held her in his arms. He'd simply been too tired to stand by himself.

His plea for her not to leave yet had been concern for his children's safety should he sleep too soundly to waken if they needed him. Tomorrow he'd pay her the wages she had coming and dismiss her. She'd be lucky if he didn't prefer charges against her.

She shifted uncomfortably on the bed and tried to bring her wavering attention back to her reading. She'd hardly gotten past the first line when there was a knock on her door. She looked at her watch. Twelve fifty-six. Who on earth could be wandering around at this hour?

"Yes," she called.

"Lark, it's Jonathan. May I come in?" The baritone voice didn't need to be identified, but for a moment she was too startled to answer.

She swallowed. "Of course, Jonathan, please do."

The door opened, and he strode in wearing brown pajamas under a maroon silk robe. What was he doing awake? She had thought he'd sleep the clock around.

"What's the matter?" she asked as she tossed her book aside and sat in the middle of the bed with the covers over her lap. He didn't look any more rested than he had when she'd left his room, and his hair was rumpled as though he'd been running his hands through it. "I thought you were asleep."

He walked over to the side of the bed and looked down at her. "I was, but I woke up again. I need to talk to you, Lark. I'd planned to wait until tomorrow after I'd had some sleep. I've done more than enough damage with words today. But I can't rest until we get this straightened out."

She tried not to cringe. Apparently he wanted her to understand that she was being dismissed, but was having trouble telling her because of the way he'd yelled at her earlier. Well, she'd make it easy for him. Then maybe he'd go away and leave her alone. She didn't want him here; he'd make her cry if he stayed any longer.

She turned her head so she wouldn't have to look at him. "If you're trying to tell me I'm fired, it's not necessary. I've already made plans to leave." Her lips were trembling, and she pressed them tightly together before she continued. "I'd intended to go tonight, but you seemed so desperately in need of sleep that I decided to stay until you woke up tomorrow."

He sank down heavily on the side of the bed, and something in his face seemed to crumble. If she didn't know better she'd think he was having as much trouble holding back tears as she was.

His hands clamped around her bare shoulders, and he shook her lightly. "You little idiot, I'm trying to apologize," he growled. "I behaved like a bastard, and I can't blame you if you never forgive me. I was just so damn mad, and when you walked in I went a little crazy. I was raging at Giselle and took it out on you. I should have at least let you explain, but I'd heard Giselle's lies so often..."

His voice trailed off, and as if he'd just realized he was shaking her, he stopped and took her face in his hands. "You don't even know what I'm babbling about, do you, love?'' His thumb caressed her lips. ''That's why I didn't want to apologize to you until I had myself under some semblance of control again, but I can't wait. I can't sleep until I know you'll be here when I wake up. That you'll at least let me try to make up to you for the awful things I said—Oh God, darling, please don't cry.''

He gathered her close and held her, but it was too late. The tears she'd been fighting for so long simply refused to be held back any longer and burst through her tight control, letting loose the trapped sobs along with them.

The storm of weeping seemed to go on and on as Jonathan held her and murmured soothing endearments. He was trying so hard to comfort her, but she could feel him trembling and knew that not all the tears mingling on their tightly pressed cheeks were hers.

Finally the tearing sobs softened to hiccups, and she lay against Jonathan's chest, spent but at peace. After a while he put his fingers under her chin and lifted her face to look up at him. His eyes were red-rimmed and when she raised her hand to his cheek his beard was damp. ''My lovely Lark,'' he said softly. ''I've missed you so. We haven't spent enough time together to begin to know each other, and still I longed for you during the day and dreamed about you at night.''

Lark raised her face as he lowered his, and when their lips met it was with a sweetness she'd never known. She was familiar with passion, but the tender, intimate caring of Jonathan's kiss was new to her. His mouth moved over hers, and her lips opened to him in total surrender.

He lowered her onto her back without breaking contact, and her arms around his neck held him to her. His tongue sought the honey of her open mouth and found the response he needed so badly. He caressed the fullness of her breasts through the satin of her nightgown, then lowered his

TAKE **4 FREE** BOOKS
WHEN YOU PEEL OFF THE BOUQUET
AND SEND IT ON THE POSTPAID CARD

Silhouette Romance®

Debbie Macomber's CHRISTMAS MASQUERADE. Jo Marie met Andrew at the Mardi Gras. By Christmas, he was introduced to her as someone else's fiancé. Why, she wondered, didn't he seem happy with his intended? Why was she back in his arms tonight? Could Andrew still be her dream man?

Arlene James' NOW OR NEVER. Mary Judith could sense new handyman Nolan Tanner was hiding a secret. She also knew one touch from him could unlock her own fiery passions. Living under the same boarding-house roof made their love seem so right — if only she could discover his secret.

Emilie Richards' GILDING THE LILY. Lesley had always held back — from success, from men, from love. Now, she had a chance to interview Travis Hagen, America's premier cartoonist. One look, and one kiss, from Travis and Lesley knew her days of holding back were gone forever.

Rita Rainville's WRITTEN ON THE WIND. Handwriting analyst Dena Trevor has to convince acting company president Brand McAllister that her expertise can unmask a company spy. Level-headed Brand has to convince himself that he is not falling in love with the beautiful Dena.

OPEN YOUR DOOR to these exciting, love-filled, full-length novels. They are yours *absolutely FREE* along with your Folding Umbrella and Mystery Gift.

AT-HOME DELIVERY. After you receive your 4 FREE books, we'll send you 6 more Silhouette Romance novels each and every month to examine FREE for fifteen days. If you decide to keep them, pay just $11.70 — with no additional charges for home delivery. If not completely satisfied, just drop us a note and we'll cancel your subscription, no questions asked. **EXTRA BONUS:** You'll also receive the Silhouette Books Newsletter FREE with every book shipment. Every issue is filled with interviews, news about upcoming books, recipes from your favorite authors, and more.

Take this beautiful
FOLDING
UMBRELLA
with your 4 FREE BOOKS
PLUS A MYSTERY GIFT

head to nibble the side of her throat and finally bury his face
in her bare shoulder.

Lark reached up and turned off the light, then cuddled
him against her and stroked her fingers through his hair.
"Don't you want to get under the covers?" she asked.

He licked the fragrant skin of her shoulder. "No. I may
be exhausted, but I'm not dead. We'd better keep the sheet
and blanket between us." His lips savored the cool softness
of her. "Good night, sweetheart, but don't expect this much
restraint the next time you let me in your bed."

She smiled in the dark. "Oh, don't worry, I won't," she
said, and drifted off to sleep in his arms.

Chapter Six

Jonathan had difficulty struggling through the layers of sleep that seemed to bury him. He was caught somewhere between a vague, undefined dream and an insistent need to awaken. Something was missing. Something important to his well-being.

He was lying on his stomach, and with effort he got control of his right arm and moved it away from him. It slid along the bed and his hand finally touched a pillow. He tried the other arm, but it moved only a few inches then dropped over the side. He felt an overwhelming and totally irrational sense of disappointment.

Then he remembered the dream.

He'd dreamed that he came to Lark in the night and she held out her arms and took him into her bed. He'd been afraid to kiss her, but when he could no longer resist she'd been warm and soft and responsive, giving as eagerly as she took. He remembered being sexually aroused—it would have been impossible not to be—but overriding it was a deep sense of peace such as he had never known. He'd somehow understood that the physical union would come in good time, but even if he never possessed her she would be his love, his life, the completion of himself.

He groaned and buried his face in the pillow. He'd been searching for her beside him in the bed, but it had been only a dream, an illusion of the mind. A way of compensating for the loneliness that had started when he took his wedding vows with Giselle seventeen years before. When he opened his eyes he would find that he was still in the depressing hotel room in Beijing, the capital of China, and was probably late for another of those interminable meetings that seemed to go nowhere...

His muscles relaxed and he dozed, then woke again with a start. What time was it, anyway, and why hadn't the alarm gone off? He rolled over and opened his eyes. The sun was streaming through the sheer blue curtains at the windows, and coming from that direction it had to be afternoon. Then his sleep-drugged mind finally focused. This wasn't the hotel room. He'd been sleeping in the bed in the room he'd assigned to Lark.

It hadn't been a dream after all. He *had* fallen asleep in her arms with his face pillowed in the softness of her breasts!

He sat up and threw his legs over the side of the bed. He was wearing pajamas and a robe and had been sleeping on top of the covers with the blue floral quilt spread over him. He didn't remember coming down here. All he remembered was Lark helping him upstairs to his room and then falling onto the king-size bed. After that was only the jumbled impressions he'd thought were a dream.

He shook his head and rubbed his hands over his face. He'd slept so soundly that he was groggy. Must have been even more tired than he'd thought. He looked at the clock radio in the bookcase headboard. One twenty-five. Good heavens! What day was it? Must be Monday. He'd landed in San Francisco on Sunday. Once he'd finally gotten to sleep he'd really made up for lost time.

He got up and went a few steps up the hall to the bathroom, where he splashed cool water on his face, brushed his teeth and combed his hair. That would at least make him presentable until he could get upstairs to shower and dress.

When he left the bathroom it occurred to him that the house was awfully quiet. He called out to Lark and Candace but there was no answer, and a search of the downstairs rooms revealed that they were empty. Lark must have gone out and taken the girls with her.

A glance into the upstairs bedrooms was equally unrewarding. The beds were made, and the rooms were neat and clean but unoccupied. He smiled. The house hadn't looked this good since his last housekeeper left. Lark was taking good care of his home...and of his daughters.

The smile disappeared as self-disgust overwhelmed him. How could he have attacked her so viciously yesterday? Not physically, of course. He hadn't touched her, but he'd shouted accusations that horrified him in retrospect. She'd looked so shocked, and then so shattered as he raged out of control. Why hadn't he gotten the facts before he started flaying her with words? When would he stop thinking that every woman was like Giselle, self-centered and uncaring?

And most important, why had she forgiven him so readily when he'd finally stumbled down to her room in the middle of the night? He now remembered waking up and feeling tormented at the way he'd treated her. His unjust censure, his refusal to apologize earlier. How could she have known how badly he wanted her forgiveness? How desperately he needed her in his arms, her lips responding to his, her body curled against him in sleep?

He grimaced and headed for the shower. He damn well should have stayed in his own bed last night. Now that he knew the taste and the feel of her, how was he going to resist the temptation to seduce her totally? Just the thought of it made his body tighten in anticipation.

Lark drove her car into the driveway, and Candace gathered up the packages while Lark unbuckled a sleepy Patty from her car seat and carried her into the kitchen. "Just bring my things up with yours," she told Candace as they started up the stairs. "We'll sort them out after I've put Patty to bed for her nap."

There was no sign of Jonathan, and she wondered if he was still in bed. She'd better check on him when she got back downstairs; he'd been sleeping for an awfully long time.

They were just a few steps from Candace's room when Jonathan came out of his bedroom farther down the hall. He was dressed in trousers and a white long-sleeved shirt with a blue tie, and carried his suit coat over his arm.

Candace hurried to him. "Hi, Dad," she said as she threw her arms around him. "You look a lot better this afternoon."

It was true, he did. His eyes sparkled as he hugged his elder daughter. "I should, after all that sleep," he said, and released her. "How's my girl? And where have you all been? I thought you'd deserted me."

Before anyone could answer, Patty came to life. "Daddy! Daddy!" she screamed, and held out her arms to him as she squirmed to get away from Lark.

Jonathan took her, and she wrapped her little arms around his neck and hung on. "Hello, baby," he said. "Hey, I think you missed your old daddy." He hugged her. "Well, I missed you every bit as much."

Lark stood apart and watched Jonathan with his daughters. She wondered if the girls had any idea how lucky they were to have such a devoted father. Her thoughts shifted to Wayne. He hadn't wanted children, didn't even like them. That was just one of the many ways in which they'd been incompatible.

She wished now that their precautions hadn't been so successful, but immediately recognized it as a selfish whim. She firmly believed that a child needed two loving parents, and Wayne would never have been the type of father she wanted her children to have. On the other hand, Jonathan . . .

She quickly turned off that thought. Jonathan Nolan had a family, and he'd made it clear that he wasn't looking for another wife. She had no intentions of getting her heart broken again. Once was enough.

She noticed that Jonathan was looking at her, and she smiled. "It's no use my trying to take her from you; she'd just cry. Do you mind putting her down for her nap?"

He flashed an answering smile. "Sure. While I'm doing that, could you fix me a sandwich or something? I'd like to leave for the office as soon as possible."

She nodded and headed downstairs while Candace followed her dad into the nursery.

Lark had the coffee made and was just sliding an omelet onto a warm plate when Jonathan came into the kitchen. "Smells good," he said, and headed for the coffeemaker. "I'm hungry."

He smelled good, too. He'd showered and shaved just before she and the children had gotten home. His hair was still damp, and his shaving lotion was fresh and sharp. "I'm not surprised," she said in the same impersonal tone he'd used. "You missed both breakfast and lunch. Do you want your Danish heated?"

He poured his coffee and took it to the table. "No," he said as he sat down. "I prefer it cold with butter."

She put the omelet in front of him, then went over to the counter and took a pastry from the bakery box she'd brought home with her. She put it on a plate and took it to him, then went to the refrigerator for the butter. "We have orange, tomato, or apple juice. Which do you prefer?"

"Apple, please, and make it a big glass." He looked up as she placed the butter on the table. "Have you had lunch?"

"Yes," she said, and went to the cupboard for a glass. "Candace and I picked Patty up from day care at noon; then we had lunch at a small restaurant Candace recommended and did some shopping before coming home. I thought you'd sleep better without all of us making noise."

She was becoming jumpier by the minute. So far he hadn't alluded to what had happened last night. Was it possible he didn't remember coming to her? He'd been awfully tired. Maybe he had no memory of waking up and seeking her out.

She put the glass of apple juice beside his coffee cup and asked, "Is there anything else you'd like?"

"Yes, there is," he said without hesitation. "I'd like for you to stop flitting around and sit down."

He stood and positioned one of the chairs right next to him at the round table. "Here." He motioned for her to sit and she did. "Can I bring you some coffee?"

"Oh, I can get it." She started to rise, but he put his hand on her shoulder and held her down.

"You just sit still and let me wait on you for a while." He took a mug from the cupboard and brought it and the coffee carafe back to the table.

After he'd filled the cups he sat down beside her. "Now, let's stop skirting the issue and talk about last night. Candace says you told her that you and I switched rooms so I could sleep without being wakened by Patty.''

Lark gulped a swallow of her coffee. "Well, I—she discovered that you weren't in your room and wanted to know where you were. I couldn't very well tell her you'd spent the night sleeping with me." Damn, she was blushing again.

The look in his eyes was soft and warm, and he raised his hand and stroked her hair back from her face. "Ah, yes, that could have been awkward, but the operative word *is* 'sleeping.'"

She shivered as he trailed his finger down her cheek and along the outline of her jaw, leaving pinpricks of pleasure in its wake. "You and I know that," she said huskily, "but I'm afraid your daughter would never have believed it."

He cupped his hand under her chin and tilted her face upward. "Smart girl, my daughter," he said, and touched his lips to hers. "I can hardly believe it myself. My age must be catching up with me."

She shifted her hand and tangled her fingers in his beard. "Not age," she whispered, "time zones." Her eyes widened. "That is, unless you found the company unexciting."

He groaned softly. "Believe me, the company was exciting, but thank God I was too exhausted to do anything about it. If I hadn't been, I wouldn't have stayed, and last night I needed you in my arms."

Again he kissed her lightly, and she moved her stroking fingers to his hair.

"I reached for you when I woke up," he said, "and I felt abandoned when you weren't there beside me."

The corners of her mouth turned up in an impish grin. "You may have forgotten, but you have a small daughter who gets up early. This morning it was six o'clock. I got out

f bed and turned off the intercom before I went to her so
ae wouldn't wake you up, too.''

He put his arms around her then and hugged her to him.
Oh, Lark,'' he said in a tone that sounded like a cross be-
veen amusement and regret. ''I'm afraid your virtue is safe
round here. How could I seduce you with a houseful of
ids keeping track of our every move? I guess I'll have to
:sign myself to living like a monk.''

He released her then and stood. ''I'll probably be late
etting home. Do you mind if we don't have dinner until
bout seven?''

He put on his suit coat and hurried off without waiting
r an answer.

Lark saw little of Jonathan during the rest of the week.
he would fix his breakfast, but then was too busy getting
atty dressed and fed to eat with him. They had dinners to-
ether with the children, but after she'd cleaned up the
itchen and he'd put Patty to bed, he would disappear into
is study with a briefcase full of papers he'd brought home
rom work, and he wouldn't come out until time for the late
ews on television. They watched that together, then re-
ired to their separate rooms for the night. He hadn't
ouched her since Monday, or said anything that could be
onsidered personal.

Meanwhile her feelings for him were growing more per-
onal every day, and she knew he wasn't as impervious to
er as he pretended to be. There was too much sensual ten-
ion between them for it to be one-sided. Her good sense
old her to get out of there as quickly as she could. She knew
hat the next time Jonathan came to her bed it wouldn't be
o sleep. She also knew that she'd welcome him uncondi-
ionally, and that was what frightened her.

Lark had never been the type to sleep around. The on
man she'd made love with was Wayne, and then only aft
they were married. She'd been raised with old-fashione
moral values, and they suited her. That's why the know
edge that she would make love with Jonathan if he asked h
was so disconcerting. It meant that her feelings for him we
neither casual nor fleeting. They were strong and deep, an
becoming more so every day.

Under other circumstances she would have welcome
these emotions. She wanted a husband and family. Her d
vorce hadn't left permanent scars, and she was willing to tr
again. Especially with a man like Jonathan, who was prac
tically the embodiment of her dream lover. He was stron
but gentle, sexier than any man had a right to be, a lovin
father, and an intelligent and successful businessman.

He was also off limits and unavailable.

Jonathan hadn't survived his divorce as well as Lark ha
survived hers. His wounds were still raw and painful. H
had never resolved his differences with Giselle, and so sh
still had the power to torment him. Even now he was bein
secretly investigated by her parents, and most damning o
all, Lark was the one doing the investigating. She'd lied t
him to get into his home and into his life. When he foun
out—and there was no doubt but that he would—he'd neve
forgive her.

On Saturday Jonathan took them on an outing through
the Avenue of the Giants, the 33-mile-long scenic highwa
through the oldest and largest of the towering redwoods
Lark had come through them on her way to Eureka, bu
she'd stayed on the newer four-lane highway instead o
turning off onto the old two-lane that wound along the un
tamed Eel River and through the deeply shaded groves o
two-thousand-year-old giants.

Candace had received permission from her father to invite Dirk Olafsson along, and Lark packed a picnic lunch complete with fried chicken, potato salad, and fresh raw vegetables and fruits.

For the first few miles of the journey through rolling hills dressed with oak, maple, madrone, and pepperwood trees, Dirk and Candace seemed uneasy, almost apprehensive, but by the time they reached the northern entrance to the Avenue of the Giants a half hour later, they realized that Lark would keep her word and not mention their indiscretion to Jonathan. Lark couldn't entirely banish a feeling of guilt at keeping this important information from Candace's father, but it was imperative that Candace know Lark trusted her. Lark was in the uncomfortable position of being caught between a rock and a hard place, but there was nothing she could do about it now.

At noon, after stopping several times to explore some of the more unusual trees, they turned west off the highway and drove deep into Rockefeller Forest, a thirteen-thousand-acre preserve, to eat their lunch at one of the picnic areas.

When they'd finished, Candace and Dirk wandered off hand in hand on one of the trails leading through tall ferns, fallen trees and the primitive environs of the redwood forest. They took Patty with them, and Jonathan called after them. "Don't be gone more than half an hour. We still have a way to go before we start back."

Lark stood and stretched. "Why don't we go for a walk, too?" she asked. "I've been sitting for so long that I feel all knotted up."

"Great idea," he answered, and reached for her hand, twining his fingers through hers. His touch was like a jolt of electricity, and Lark had the feeling that it had fused their hands together for all time. *What nonsense,* she admonished herself silently, but she was too happy to rein in her soaring imagination.

"I feel so...so insignificant," she said with a sigh as they wandered down a different trail. "Some of these trees have been here for thousands of years. It's hard to believe that the one we saw earlier has survived fire, lightning, flood and the ax and is still growing."

He grinned down at her. "Believe it, my little skeptic. These redwoods are almost indestructible. Some of them were old before Christ was born!"

Lark was fascinated by the height of the gigantic trees, some over three hundred feet. In order to see the tops she was forced to tip her head back as she walked. In time the inevitable happened and she tripped over a tangle of roots in the path. Jonathan caught her before she could fall, then kept his arm around her waist as they walked. She snuggled happily against his side.

"We mustn't wander too far," she said finally. "You told Candace and Dirk not to be gone more than half an hour."

"We'll turn back in a minute," he said, then changed the subject. "What do you think of Dirk?"

Lark was surprised. "He seems like a nice young man," she said cautiously.

"Did he and Candace spend much time together while I was gone?" Jonathan asked.

"Well, actually no." Lark chose her words carefully. "She brought him to the house a few days after you left, and asked if she could go to a rock concert with him that night. I'm afraid I didn't make myself very popular with either of them when I said no, but you hadn't said anything about her dating and I didn't know whether or not you'd approve." Lark wasn't lying; she just wasn't telling him everything.

"I'm sorry. The boy was away at the time I left, and I just didn't think. I've been letting her go out with him, but she

as to be in no later than midnight. I like Dirk, he comes
from a good family, but I don't altogether trust him with my
daughter." He chuckled. "Comes to that, I'll admit—
mit that I wouldn't trust any boy his age with my daughter.
I was eighteen myself once, and I wish to God someone had
put the skids under me."

He stopped walking, and Lark looked up at him. The
laughter was gone, and there was no amusement in his
expression now. It was pensive.

He leaned against the big redwood beside them and
turned Lark so that he held her full length against him. In
her sneakers she was short enough that her cheek fit into the
hollow below his shoulder, and she sighed contentedly. She
might as well enjoy this. It would have to last her a lifetime. Very soon now she would have to confess to Jonathan her real reason for taking the job as his housekeeper.

"Were you really such a terror?" she asked against his
knit shirt.

His hands moved slowly over her back. "No more than
most teenagers, but that was the year I started dating Gi-
elle. She was sixteen, the same age Candace is now. Two
years later we got married because she was pregnant. From
then until now, the only thing we had in common was our
daughter. I don't want that for Candace, even if I have to
seem unduly strict."

So Jonathan's marriage had been of the proverbial
shotgun type. Lark felt a wave of sympathy for him, although she certainly couldn't consider him blameless. How
much better it would have been if, in the natural cycle of life,
the mating instinct had been deferred until men and women
were old enough and wise enough to deal with it responsi-
bly. If they could go directly from childhood to adulthood
without the painful adolescent years, that purgatory period

when it was so easy to ruin whole lives with one careles
mistake.

Since he had brought up the subject, Lark had a ques
tion that was none of her business, but the answer was im
portant to her. "Would you have married Giselle if sh
hadn't been pregnant?"

He didn't hesitate. "No, I wouldn't have. Years later
during one of our incessant quarrels, she told me that she'
deliberately stopped taking the pill because she'd sensed
was losing interest and would soon break off with her. Sh
was right on both counts, but when I knew there was going
to be a baby I had no choice. I couldn't allow my child to b
born without a father."

She snuggled closer and wrapped her arms around hi
waist. "How sad," she said. "Now that I think of it, I'm
afraid I more or less forced my husband into marriage too."

She felt Jonathan stiffen. "I thought you said you didn'
have children," he rasped.

"Oh, I don't," she hastened to assure him. "Actually i
was because I *wasn't* in any danger of getting pregnant tha
Wayne married me. I was eighteen, but he was a grown man,
twenty-two years old and a senior in college. I was in love
with him—or thought I was—but I'd been taught that a gir
shouldn't give herself to a man until he was her husband.
Wayne finally understood that the only way he was going to
get me into bed was to marry me, so he did."

Jonathan bent his head and caressed her temple with his
lips. "I can understand his problem. You're an awfully
tempting armful. What I don't understand is how he could
let you go once he had you. You feel so good cuddled
against me like this."

His hand moved under her cotton sweater, and she shivered as he caressed her bare flesh. "All the time I was in
China I had trouble falling asleep, and when I finally did I

was restless. I told myself I was just lonesome, and I was, but what I wouldn't admit was that I was lonesome for you. It didn't make sense. I didn't know you well enough to miss you, but I did. Then, when I finally got home and you took pity on me for being such a jackass and let me in your bed, I couldn't deny it any longer. You curled against me in sleep, and for the first time since I'd left home I was content."

Lark stroked his chest through his shirt. "I didn't take pity on you that night," she murmured. "I wanted you to sleep with me."

He moaned softly and crushed her to him as he searched for and found her willing mouth. His tongue coupled with hers, and his hands cupped her buttocks and lifted her until she fit intimately where he needed her to be. She stood on tiptoe and clung to him, eagerly responding to the kiss that became more and more demanding.

One hand returned to her bare back beneath the sweater, while the other one held her to him. He unhooked her bra, and his palm brushed the side of her breast, then slid beneath it and cradled it gently while his fingers teased the hardened peak.

"Have you any idea how often I've lain awake at night aching for the touch of your soft breast in my hand?" he murmured against the side of her mouth. "I didn't think it could possibly be as perfect as I imagined it to be, but it's even better. Has anyone ever told you that you have a bosom that could drive a man out of his mind?"

She rubbed the back of his neck in a tender massage. "The subject has been mentioned, but I always figured it was just a line," she answered dreamily.

"It's not a line," he said. "If you have any doubt, I'll prove it." His hand on her bottom pushed her even closer.

She'd been well aware of his arousal, and of her own. Her breasts were heavy and throbbing, and so were other, more

intimate parts of her. She wanted to put her hands under hi
shirt and touch his bare skin as he was touching hers; to ex
plore the firm muscles that bulged across his shoulders
chest and waist.

She wondered if he still worked cutting timber on occa
sion. Whatever he did to keep fit, it certainly was effective
The tightness of his jeans exposed his muscular thighs, and
the belly that pressed so intimately against her was flat and
hard.

Again his mouth sought hers and she opened to him, in
viting his entry. Somewhere deep inside her the small voice
of her conscience was struggling to be heard, but she shut it
out. Nothing mattered but the pulsing need that raced
through her like a flame. Jonathan wanted her and, oh God,
how she wanted him.

But is that enough for you? The voice was getting
stronger. *Will a quick roll on the floor of the forest be worth
a lifetime of guilt and remorse?*

She struggled against the voice. She was an adult. She'd
been married. There was no reason why she shouldn't make
love with a man if she wanted to.

But not this man.

Her arms tightened around Jonathan's neck. She
wouldn't listen. She wouldn't.

*You aren't playing fair with Jonathan. In a few days he'll
know the truth about you, and he'll hate you all the more
for tempting him with a love that can never be. You'll hurt
him even more cruelly than Giselle did, and you'll have done
it deliberately.*

With a sob, Lark tore her lips from his. For a moment he
tried to recapture them, but she turned her head away. "No,
Jonathan. We can't. The others. Candace. They'll be waiting for us.''

Gradually his hold on her loosened as he struggled to control his breathing. "Yes, of course," he said finally, and dropped his arms to his sides. "You go on back. I—I need a few minutes to calm down."

He caught her lightly by the shoulders and brushed her mouth with his own. "Lark, we have a problem," he said raggedly.

She trembled beneath his hands and lips. She wanted to throw her arms around him and take up where they'd left off, and to hell with the future. Instead she stepped back. "I know." Her voice was unsteady. "And it's even more complicated than you imagine."

She turned and walked away, knowing she could never allow this to happen again. The next time she wouldn't stop him.

Chapter Seven

Lark arranged to take the following day, Sunday, off since Jonathan was home now to stay with the girls. She spent it with Rob and Melanie, and was greeted with hugs and kisses from both the adults and the little boys when she arrived. It was still early and they insisted that she have breakfast with them. She wasn't about to turn down bacon, eggs, pancakes and a fresh fruit compote.

For a while afterward she played with her small nephews, wrestling and tumbling around on the floor with them like the tomboy she used to be. Rob grinned and said to Melanie, "I used to wonder if that sister of mine was ever going to start acting like a girl. She used to tag along after me and my buddies every chance she got. Have you any idea how embarrassing it is to have a little sister who's a better pitcher than you are?"

Lark guffawed. "Darn right I was, and if I'd been born a few years later I'd have been in Little League."

"Did you play baseball, Aunt Lark?" asked five-year-old Bobby, as Tommy, age three, chased a beach ball down the hall.

"Sure did," Lark bragged, "and when you guys get old enough for Little League I'll come back and teach you how to pitch and swing a bat."

Lark got up off the floor and headed for the kitchen. "If you don't mind, I'm going to have that third cup of coffee now," she said over her shoulder.

A few minutes later Rob, Lark and Melanie were relaxing in the living room with coffee while the boys played on their swing set in the backyard. Lark sighed. "How I wish I could take Bobby and Tommy home with me. Patty would love to play with them."

Rob raised one eyebrow. "*Home* to Jonathan Nolan's house? Lark, are you getting more involved over there than you should?"

Lark blinked. It was true, she'd been thinking of Jonathan's house as home lately. She hadn't been there three weeks yet, but already she felt a part of the Nolan family. That was another of the many mistakes she'd been making.

"I—I'm afraid so," she said, and looked down at her coffee. "It would be difficult not to love Candace and Patty."

"And Jonathan?"

Lark continued to toy with the mug. "Jonathan is a kind and attractive man, but he's been gone a lot of the time." She didn't sound very convincing.

"Stop hedging," Rob said firmly. "Is there something going on between you and Jonathan Nolan?"

"He's been a perfect gentleman, if that's what you mean."

"That's not what I'm asking," her brother countered, "since I've no idea what you consider a gentleman. Do you mean he still calls you Mrs. Bancroft and treats you like his grandmother, or are you saying he never makes love to you without asking first?''

Lark slammed her mug down on the coffee table. "Dammit, Rob, you don't need to be crude!''

"Sorry." Rob slumped back in his chair. "That was uncalled for, but don't forget that it's *my* business that's at stake here. I've no intention of losing my license because of unethical practices. If you're emotionally involved with Jon, I want to know it.''

Lark, too, made an effort to relax. Rob was right, she was working for him and he was entitled to the truth. "I'm afraid I am...emotionally involved with Jonathan, but not physically. He doesn't want a furtive love affair any more than I do, but if I stay in that house much longer I can't guarantee that it won't happen.''

Rob muttered an indelicate oath. "Are you in love with him?''

Lark threaded her fingers through her luxuriant brown hair. "I hope not," she said, and meant it. "Jonathan is bitter about women in general and Giselle in particular. When he finds out what I am...what I've done...he'll never forgive me. That's not conjecture, it's hard, cold fact. He doesn't want to feel anything for me, but he does and he fights against it. It's the same with me, but when he touches me all my good sense evaporates.''

Rob was up now and pacing back and forth. "Why didn't you come to me with this before? I distinctly remember asking you earlier if you were getting too fond of Jon, and you denied it.''

Lark shrugged. "At that time he was in China, and I thought it was just a one-sided attraction. I could have handled it, but when he came to me the night he got home

nd . . .'' She choked on a sob, and a tear rolled down one
heek.

Rob swore and stopped directly in front of her. "I don't
vant you to go back to that house. I'll send someone to pick
ıp your clothes and tell Jonathan that you're leaving town.
Ve can say there's been an illness in your family.''

She shook her head. "I can't do that, Rob. There's no one
lse to look after Candace and Patty. Besides, I couldn't just
valk away. I've committed enough sins against Jonathan.
'm not going to add desertion just when he needs me.''

"And just when do you think he's going to stop needing
ou?'' Rob growled. "You've been married; how come
ou're so uninformed where men are concerned? His need
or you will grow stronger every day you're in his home,
aking care of his children and tempting the hell out of him.
You'll only make it harder for him if you go back.''

Lark suspected Rob was at least partially right, but the
idea of just walking away and never seeing Jonathan and his
daughters again was unthinkable. She couldn't do it,
vouldn't do it; it was asking too much. She'd set Jonathan
ıp for enough pain as it was. She couldn't let him think she
vas totally uncaring. The least she could do was face him
ınd apologize when the showdown came.

"I'm sorry, but I don't agree," she said, and her tone was
determined. "I can't leave until I've confessed the truth to
ıim and tried to make him understand how sorry I am for
deceiving him.''

"Now wait a minute." Rob sat down on the sofa beside
Lark. "You can't blow your cover and expose this whole
nvestigation. The Ulrics would sue me. After all, they're the
ones who instigated it, and it's their money that's paying for
t. This has to remain confidential, at least until I can talk
:hem into dropping it. Even then I'd have to have their permission to tell Jon about it, and you know damn well they're

not going to give that. Jon would probably never let them
see their granddaughters again, and who could blame him?"

Lark felt a curious sense of relief. She'd been given a lit
tle time. At least she didn't have to go back today and tel
him her guilty secret. "We seem to have come to an im
passe," she said to Rob. "I can't leave without telling Jon
athan the truth, and you can't let me do that. Have you any
idea when the Ulrics will be back from Alaska?"

"Not for sure, but it should be any day now. Don't count
on them dropping the investigation, though."

She picked up her mug and swallowed what was left of her
now cool coffee. "If we could only find Giselle. If her par
ents knew where she was and that she was all right there
wouldn't be any need to tell Jonathan anything about my
part in finding her. Then I could just tell him I'd changed
my mind about living in Eureka and leave. At least he'd re
member me kindly."

Rob snorted. "Dream on if that's what you want to think
but we both know you're not going to get out of this so
painlessly. I've got an operative tracking Giselle, but so fai
all he's learned is that she headed south out of town or
Highway one-o-one, spent one night in a cheap motel in the
San Joaquin valley, and a month later worked for a week in
a bar in Los Angeles. The bartender said she talked about
going to Las Vegas, but we haven't been able to find her
there. Have you gotten Jon to talk about her?"

Lark's conscience pricked her. She hadn't even at
tempted to question him about his wife's disappearance.
This situation was impossible. She felt guilty if she did
question him, and guilty if she didn't. "No," she said. "He
says very little about her, and then only in a roundabout
way. He's admitted that they were unhappy and quarreled
a lot, but that's all." She didn't consider it necessary to tell

Rob that Jonathan had only married Giselle because she was pregnant with his child.

"How about Candace?" Rob asked. "What does she have to say about her mother?"

Lark looked away. "I—I haven't asked her. It seems like such an ... an invasion of privacy to pry into an unsuspecting sixteen-year-old girl's thoughts."

"Now look, Lark." Rob's tone was stern. "Either you do the job you were sent to do, or else get off the case. You know better than to let your personal feelings interfere with getting the information you need. You're not doing Jonathan *or* Candace a favor by dragging your heels and letting this investigation run on longer than is necessary. If they know something, then it's up to you to find out what it is and tell me."

Lark knew she deserved the scolding. "I'm sorry," she said, "but it hasn't been as easy as I thought it would be. I had a rather serious disciplinary problem with Candace while her father was out of the country, and she barely spoke to me all the time he was gone. We've gotten that straightened out now, though, so I'll talk to her."

It was eleven o'clock and had been dark for a long time when Lark left her brother's house to return to Jonathan's. Both of Jonathan's cars were in the garage, and the light had been left on for her, a thoughtful gesture she appreciated. The interior of the house was also lit, but everything was quiet. Lark wondered if Jonathan had gone to bed, and she was careful not to make any noise as she turned off the kitchen light and headed for the hallway.

"Lark? Is that you?" It was Jonathan's voice coming from the living room.

Before she could answer he stepped into the hall. "Well, I see you finally decided to come home." He was wearing jeans and a partially unbuttoned shirt, and she detected a definite note of sarcasm in his tone.

"I—I hadn't realized you expected me back at any specific time," she said, and regretted the quiver in her voice. After all, it was her day off. She didn't owe him any explanations. "Was there a problem while I was gone?"

"Yes, there was a problem," he said as he took her arm and escorted her into the living room. "I was worried about you." He sounded more angry than worried. "You left before breakfast this morning, and it's now after eleven o'clock at night. As far as I know you haven't either friends or relatives living in the area, so where have you been?"

Lark bristled. She'd lived on her own for four years, and she wasn't used to having to account to anyone for her absences. Her indignation came through loud and clear as she said, "I'm a big girl now, Jonathan, and it's none of your business what I do on my days off."

"Were you with a man?" he grated.

Lark was flabbergasted, then incensed. "Since you've just indicated that I have no friends in the area, I assume you're asking me if I picked up some stranger off the street and went home with him." Her voice crackled with fury.

Jonathan looked startled but didn't back down. "I wouldn't have put it so crudely, but I guess that is what I want to know."

"Well, don't hold your breath, because I've no intention of answering." She was shaking with outrage. "Think what you want. I don't give a damn." She turned abruptly and stomped off to her room, where she slammed the door behind her.

Lark spent a sleepless night alternating between pacing the floor in a rage and curling up on the bed in anguish be-

...use Jonathan could think her capable of such gross be-
...avior.

Although she no longer kept the intercom tuned into
...atty's room since Jonathan had told her he'd take care of
...is little daughter during the time he was home, she always
...t her alarm for six-thirty so she could get up and fix
...reakfast for him before he left for work. This morning she
...nored the alarm and stayed in bed until there was a knock
...n her door and Jonathan called, "Lark, I have to leave
...ow. May I bring Patty in?"

She hadn't thought of the possibility that he'd come
...eking her in her bedroom. She sat up and brushed her
...ngled hair back from her face. "Yes. Come in," she said.
... quick glance downward satisfied her that although her
...al blue nightgown was low cut it was opaque and not too
...vealing.

The door opened, and he entered leading his small
...aughter by the hand. He was dressed in a freshly pressed
...lue suit and crisp white shirt, but his face was pale and
...rawn and he didn't look as if he'd gotten any more sleep
...an she had.

Her gaze collided for a moment with his before she looked
...way and turned her attention to Patty. The child was
...ressed in clean pink overalls with a ruffle-edged bib over a
...olor-coordinated striped blouse.

Lark held out her arms. "Come on, honey. You can get
... my bed while I dress."

Patty ran to the bed and climbed up into Lark's arms.
...ark hugged the little one to her, then realized that Jona-
...an had followed and was standing beside the bed.

She didn't look up as he spoke. "Lark, I'm sorry. I didn't
...ean... You must know I wouldn't think..." He shifted
...rom one foot to the other. "Look, we've got to talk. Will
...ou talk to me tonight?"

She nodded, still not looking at him. "Yes. I think w
both have things to say."

For a moment she felt the pressure of his hand caressin
her hair; then he was gone.

The atmosphere at dinner that evening was tense an
strained, although both Lark and Jonathan tried to rela
and lighten it for the sake of Candace and Patty. Appar
ently they were successful because both girls chattered on a
usual, Candace about her duties at the gift shop of the lc
cal hospital where she worked as a volunteer candy stripe
and Patty about the swimming lesson Lark had taken her t
that morning. Jonathan and Lark listened attentivel
commenting where appropriate, while looking everywher
but at each other.

After they'd finished eating, Jonathan took Patty up
stairs to bathe her and put her to bed while Lark cleaned u
in the kitchen. On his return from China, Jonathan had de
creed that since Lark cooked dinner, Candace was to do th
cleaning up afterward, but tonight the girl was going to
movie with Dirk, so Lark relieved her of the duty.

Besides, Lark needed something to do to keep her min
off the talk she and Jonathan were to have. It was plain tha
he intended to apologize for his outburst the night before
but what then? Would he fire her? The thought brough
chills of apprehension, even though it would solve he
problem with her conscience. Or would he take her to bed
The chills turned to heat, and she tried to shut out the fan
tasy of his hard naked body pressed intimately against he
soft one.

Dirk arrived for Candace just as Jonathan was comin
downstairs, and Lark joined them in the entryway to sa
goodbye as the young couple left. Jonathan shut the doo
and turned to Lark, but he didn't look at her directly. In

stead he took her arm and turned her toward the den. "Come, Lark," he said, "it's time for us to straighten out some of our misunderstandings."

His touch sent tingles radiating up and down her arm. He'd changed from his business suit into tan slacks and a brown knit shirt, open at the throat, but the more informal style of dress hadn't relaxed him. Lark could feel his tension responding to her own.

In the den he seated her on the leather sofa that faced the fireplace, then walked over to the French doors leading to the redwood deck and stood with his back to the room, looking out over the breathtaking view of Humbolt Bay. "I owe you an apology," he said, still not turning around. "The problem is that I've had to apologize to you so often since we met, that I'm beginning to wonder what's wrong with me. I don't usually slam doors on people, or yell at them, or insult them, so why am I at my worst with you?"

It wasn't a question that required an answer, and Lark sat with her feet tucked under her full, multicolored cotton skirt while Jonathan ran his hand through his dark hair in a gesture of frustration. "When you left yesterday without saying where you were going, I assumed you'd be back early. By dinnertime I was concerned, and when you finally came in I was pacing the floor and wondering if I should call the police. When I knew that you were all right I was so relieved, and felt like such a fool for being concerned, that I just blew up and said all the wrong things."

Lark couldn't sit there any longer letting him apologize because he'd cared enough to worry about her. She got up and went to him. "Jonathan, I'm sorry," she said, and put her hand on his arm. "I should have called to let you know I'd be late, but I had no idea you'd care."

He turned then and took her in his arms. "Oh, I care," he said softly as he rubbed his bearded cheek in her fra-

grant hair. "That's the problem. I don't want to worry
about a woman ever again; to wonder where she is, who
she's with, what she's doing. I had enough of that with Giselle to last a lifetime, and I'm not going to open myself to
that kind of torment again."

"Do you still worry about Giselle?" Lark wasn't thinking as a private investigator now, but as a jealous woman.

"Of course I do," he said bitterly. "I haven't any idea
where she is. You've probably been told by now that she's
disappeared. We had a vicious quarrel one morning, and the
next day she was gone and hasn't been seen or heard from
since."

The peace officer in Lark began to surface. Jonathan and
his ex-wife had quarreled just before she disappeared! As far
as she knew he'd never told anyone else that. Lark raised her
head and looked at him. "What did you quarrel about?"
She hated herself for asking, but she had to know.

He shook his head and pressed her face back against his
shoulder. "It doesn't matter. We were involved in a custody battle at the time, and we were both bitter and angry.
She got the perfect revenge, though. For a year I haven't
known whether she's dead or alive. The police think I may
have had something to do with her disappearance, and her
parents are sure of it. It's like living in purgatory, never
knowing whether I'll be moving on to heaven or hell."

Her arms tightened around his slender waist, and he cuddled her closer. "Oh sweetheart," she whispered, her lips
caressing him through his shirt. "I'm so sorry. What about
Candace? Has she any idea where her mother is?"

"No." His tone was heavy with disgust. "Giselle fought
me at every turn when I tried to get custody of our daughters, but then she just walked away from them without even
saying goodbye. At least if she ever returns I won't have to
worry about the judge giving them back to her."

For a few minutes they stood silently in the circle of each other's arms, their thoughts troubled.

Any doubts Lark may have had about Jonathan's innocence of the charges his ex-in-laws had brought against him had been banished. She knew he was telling the truth. He didn't know where Giselle was, and it worried him and made his life miserable. Even after being divorced for two years he still felt responsible for her. Lark's admiration for this man was almost as deep as her love.

Yes, love. She might as well face it, she was in love with Jonathan Nolan. She hadn't planned it or wanted it, but it had happened, and the only way she knew how to deal with it was to accept it and go on from there. She'd walked into his little trap with her eyes wide open, and now that it was sprung she had nobody but herself to blame.

Now the only thing she could do for him was to leave before they became any more involved with each other. She could feel his heart beating against her breast, and she was aware of his arousal as he held her close against him. He fought against it, but he wanted her, needed her, almost as much as she wanted and needed him.

Jonathan clung to Lark's soft yielding body like a lifeline and berated himself for his weakness. He'd been steeling himself all day for this encounter, telling himself she was just another woman and that a woman was the last thing he needed in his life. By the time he'd put Patty to bed he'd thought he had everything under control.

Control, hah! The first time she touched him he caved in and took her in his arms, and now he wasn't sure he'd ever be able to let go of her. She was so warm, and so sweet, and she was driving him crazy with desire. If he didn't send her away soon he was going to take her to bed, and he didn't need a soothsayer to tell him that he'd do anything to keep her once that happened.

He had no choice; he had to send her away. Not only for himself, but also for his children. Tonight when he'd put Patty to bed she'd given him a kiss to give to "Mommy," and she'd meant Lark. The child had already been deserted by one Mommy. He had to protect her from a repeat experience when Lark left.

He didn't dare deliver the kiss. He knew that if he started he wouldn't be able to stop.

Lark was the first to break the silence, and when she did it was with another of the lies she was getting so good at telling. "I do have friends in the area, Jonathan." She raised her head and nuzzled his bearded jaw. "A woman I went to high school with lives in Crescent City with her husband and little boy, and I drove up there to spend the day with them."

As usual her lie was mixed with the truth. She did have a high school chum in Crescent City, but she hadn't seen her in years.

Jonathan shivered as she continued the tender assault on his jawline. "Lark, my God, if you keep that up I'm going to lose what little restraint I have left," he groaned, and put her away from him. "Let's sit down. I have something to say to you, and it just gets harder the longer I put it off."

Lark went back to the couch, but Jonathan took a chair off to one side. He got right to the point. "I was married seventeen years ago, and it was the biggest mistake I ever made. Oh, I suppose we had some happy times together, but I can't remember them. All I remember is the bickering, the jealousy, the rage, and the bitter quarrels. Even after we were divorced it didn't stop. Twice I filed for custody of the children, and twice Giselle fought me with all her feminine wiles and family influence even though she didn't really want them. She wanted to get back at me for finally walking out on her, and that was the way she could do it that would hurt the most."

Lark wondered how a woman like Giselle Nolan could justify her selfish actions to herself. She probably didn't have a conscience to worry about.

Jonathan sighed. "I realize that I was at fault too. It takes two to break up a marriage, and we were both young and spoiled only children who were used to having our own way. In the beginning I was resentful at being forced into a commitment I didn't want, and I didn't try too hard to hide it. We hadn't been getting along before the wedding, and it sure didn't get any better afterward."

He shifted position uneasily. "What I'm trying to tell you is that now, for the first time in my adult life, I have things on a fairly even keel and I'm pretty much content. I'm free of the bonds of an unhappy marriage and I have custody of my children. I'm not interested in committing myself to a woman ever again."

Lark had suspected that this was what he was leading up to, but even so it was like a sharp blow to her midsection. He had said he cared for her, but obviously not enough to want her in his life.

He paused as if waiting for her to say something, but when she didn't he continued. "I'm going to go back on a promise I made to you, Lark, and I'm truly sorry. I told you that if you'd stay with the girls while I was in China you could have the position of housekeeper for as long as you wanted it, but surely it's obvious that such a thing would never work. The problem that I was sure would arise has. I can't keep my hands off you. If you stay here much longer I'm going to make love to you, and that would be disastrous for both of us."

His softly spoken words battered Lark, and she winced in an involuntary effort to ward off the pain. He was firing her. Why was she finding it so painful? This was the best thing that could have happened, a perfect way out for her. She could resign at Jonathan's request and he'd never have to know why she was really there. She'd tell him she understood, assure him that she agreed with him, and leave.

Instead she was appalled to hear herself say defensively, "What makes you so sure I'd make love with you?"

He looked at her squarely then, and she saw the torment in his eyes. "Because you melt in my arms and return my kisses and caresses with such fire." His voice was ragged. "We're both caught up in feelings we won't be able to control much longer, and I'm not going to take advantage of your warm and vulnerable nature. You've recently been divorced. I know how traumatic that can be, and it's natural for you to seek male...approval...to reassure yourself that you're still desirable."

Lark's eyes widened, and her pain was replaced with anger as she grated, "You think all I want is sex?"

"Lark, stop that!" Jonathan jumped to his feet and began to pace between the couch and the fireplace. "That's not what I meant and you know it. You told me your husband left you for another woman. That would be a blow to any woman's pride, and my obvious interest in you must be something of a balm."

Lark opened her mouth to protest, but he didn't allow an interruption. "If you were a different type of woman I'd be happy to have a temporary affair with you, but that's not for you and we both know it. You'd just be hurt all over again when I walked away, and I would walk away, Lark. I'm deadly serious about never marrying again."

Lark slumped against the back of the couch. In the beginning she'd intimated to Jonathan that she was only recently divorced, so she couldn't blame him for coming to erroneous conclusions. He had no way of knowing that she'd long ago resolved the damage Wayne had inflicted on her pride.

He was right about one thing, though. If they became lovers and then he dropped her, it would destroy her. She'd always known there was no future for her with Jonathan Nolan. If it made it easier on him to think he was protecting her in some way, then she wouldn't argue.

She tried to force some conviction in her tone as she said, "Okay, Jonathan, you're probably right. I'll clear out in the morning."

He frowned. "I didn't mean you had to leave immediately. You're welcome to stay here until you've found another position."

She shook her head. "No, I—I'm going back to Phoenix."

He looked startled. "You mean back to your ex-husband?" he asked tightly.

"Oh, no." She couldn't let him think that. "I believe I told you once that Wayne had remarried. There's nothing between us anymore, but all my family and friends are there and I miss them. My dad has a heart condition, and since I've no ties here it's best that I go home."

She pushed herself up out of the comfortable sofa and turned away from him. "If you'll excuse me, I'll go up and start packing."

Jonathan watched her as she walked slowly out of the room. He hadn't expected this. He'd assumed she would stay with them until she'd found another job, or until he'd found another housekeeper. It had never occurred to him that he wouldn't have time to get used to her leaving.

Let her go, dammit! He planted his feet firmly on the floor. *It's best this way. Get it over quickly. A nice clean break. It's good that she's going to Arizona. She'll be totally out of your reach then.*

"Lark!" The distraught cry escaped him before he could force it back, and without ever willing it he tore out of the room and up the hall toward the entryway.

Lark was halfway up the stairs when she heard her name shouted from the den. She turned and saw Jonathan bounding up the stairs after her. He grabbed her by the shoulders, and his fingers dug into her soft flesh. For a moment he held her away from him; then gradually his hands slid down her arms and circled her slender waist.

He drew her to him and held her close. They were both trembling. "I can't let you go so abruptly," he said huskily. "Stay with us until I find another housekeeper. Maybe we can work something out. I can't keep you in my house much longer, but neither can I let you go completely. I know it's asking a lot, sweetheart, but give me a little time."

Lark could hear the anguished uncertainty in his tone, and she put her arms around his neck and snuggled against him. Her mind was screaming warnings. *Don't let him do this to you. Don't do it to yourself. You've got the perfect out now, take it. If you stay, Jonathan will break your heart, and probably his own in the process. He'll hate you if he finds out you've been investigating him. Leave now while you can part friends.*

Once more she resolutely shut out the voice of her conscience, and she said the one thing guaranteed to muddy up her entire future. "I'll stay if you want me to, Jonathan, but I'd be doing you a bigger favor if I left right now."

His hold on her tightened, and he turned his head so that his lips brushed her forehead. "Kiss me good night, Lark," he whispered.

Without hesitation, she raised her mouth to his. Maybe, she told herself, a long time in the future, when he could

gain think of her without loathing, he would remember
ow eagerly she'd responded to his kisses and would know
hat she had indeed loved him.

Chapter Eight

The next morning Candace slept in and hadn't come down yet when Jonathan left for work. Lark dressed Patty and drove her to the day care center she now only attended on Monday, Wednesday, and Friday mornings, then stopped at the supermarket on her way home.

It was a beautiful, warm sunshiny day, and as she let herself into the kitchen from the garage, she hummed a catchy tune that had been playing on the car radio. Candace was sitting at the table dressed in worn jeans and a faded yellow T-shirt, with a glass of orange juice in front of her.

Lark glanced at her and smiled. "Good morning, sleepy-head. Did you enjoy the movie last night?"

"It was okay," Candace said in a dull monotone.

Lark paused in the act of emptying the grocery sack. There was pure misery in the girl's tone. What on earth had happened?

She turned and took a good look at Candace. Her hair was uncombed, her face was puffy and her expressive brown eyes were red-rimmed. "Honey, what's the matter?" Lark moved from the cabinets and sat down beside Candace.

Candace looked down at the table. "Nothing," she muttered.

"I don't mean to pry," Lark said, "but you look like you've been crying most of the night." Suddenly a disturbing thought occurred to her. "I didn't hear you come in. Were you late? Did your father scold you?"

Candace shook her head. "No, I was in by eleven-thirty." Her voice quivered. "It was Dirk and I who quarreled."

"I see," Lark said, and she truly did understand. She remembered all too well the exaggerated emotions of teenage infatuation. "Do you want to tell me what you and Dirk quarreled about?" She put her hand over Candace's where it lay on the table.

The girl grabbed her hand away and glared at Lark with fresh tears trickling down her ravaged cheeks. "He—he says we're th-through. He's not g-going to take me out anymore, and it—it's all your fault." She put her hands to her face and sobbed.

Lark gasped. Oh dear God, what had she done now? Couldn't she do anything right around here? She tried so hard to please, and yet she was always being blamed for something.

"What did I do?" she asked. "How was it my fault?"

"It—it doesn't matter now. He—he says I'm too immature for him. He wants a woman, not a child." Candace continued to sob.

"Then he should date a woman," Lark snapped, more to herself than to Candace. "Look, Candace, I can't help you if I don't know what's happened. If I did or said something to bring this on, I think I have a right to know, don't you?"

Candace took her hands from her face and looked at Lark. "You made such a big fuss over finding us kissing in my bedroom. You'd think we were in bed together the way you acted." Her voice rose in accusation as she spoke. "After that I felt guilty every time he touched me."

"And just where was he touching you?" Lark kept her tone low and gentle.

Candace's pale face turned crimson. "We haven't done anything—anything wrong," she blurted.

Lark knew she had to tread carefully. She raised her hand and brushed a strand of untidy hair away from Candace's wet cheek. "I'm sure you haven't, honey, but don't you know what it does to an eighteen-year-old boy when you let him touch your breasts, or legs, or maybe other places."

Candace shook her head vigorously. "No. No other places." Lark suppressed a smile. Jonathan's daughter really was an innocent child. Lark didn't want her innocence lost until she was mature enough to make that decision for herself, and not under the pressure of an overeager teenage boy.

"I believe you," Lark said, "but boys reach the peak of their virility at that age, and they can't always control their feelings. Girls who let them take liberties that arouse them, and then say no, might be forced. At best they'll be considered a tease."

Candace gasped. "How did you know—," she said, then clasped her hand over her mouth.

Now Lark was thoroughly alarmed. "You mean Dirk forced you?"

"No! Oh, no." Again Candace shook her head vigorously. "I meant he called me a tease."

Lark almost collapsed with relief and decided she'd better get right to the point. "Do you want to make love with Dirk, Candace?"

Candace looked startled. Clearly she hadn't expected such a blunt question. "Well I, uh, not really, but he says—"

"Never mind what he says. I'm asking what you want. Do *you* want to go to bed with him?"

Candace thought for a minute. "Sometimes I think I do, but then I get scared. I know Dad would be furious if he ever found out, and I—I might get pregnant."

"Yes, you might. Contraceptives aren't one hundred percent effective, and some boys don't like to use them." Lark took Candace's hand again, and this time she didn't pull away. "Sweetheart, you're a lovely young woman; you have your whole future ahead of you. Don't rush it. If Dirk wants to break off your friendship just because you won't sleep with him, then I wonder if he's really the kind of boy you want to go out with."

"He says he loves me," Candace said anxiously. "He says if I loved him I'd let him . . . you know."

Lark choked back the coarse oath that came to her lips. Were girls still falling for that old nonsense? "Men have been using that line ever since they stopped dragging their women back to the cave by the hair and started asking first. Just remember, it works both ways. If he really loved you, he wouldn't try to intimidate you into a relationship you aren't ready for."

Candace was silent. "I never thought of that," she finally said.

"Then think about it. And remember that you don't have to give yourself to any man until you're sure it's what you want, and that it's right for you. Be discriminating, Candace. The most precious gift you can give a man is your virginity. I hope you'll save it for the one who is special enough to be your husband."

Candace nodded thoughtfully. "You're right. You know, I've been so afraid Dirk would stop seeing me if I didn't give in to him pretty soon, that I didn't even realize he was the one who was wrong, not me." She shrugged. "I don't need him. In fact, he's been sort of a pain lately, always sulking and making me feel guilty."

Lark chuckled. "As the saying goes, 'you've come a long way, baby.' Now, why don't you run upstairs and wash your face, then go back to bed and try to sleep. I don't imagine you got much of that last night."

It was one-thirty in the afternoon before Lark heard Candace moving around upstairs. She'd slept soundly for almost four hours, and Lark hoped she was refreshed in spirit as well as body.

Apparently she was. When she came downstairs she was wearing white shorts and shirt and carrying her tennis racket. Her hair was brushed to a glistening sheen and tied back with a white scarf, and the despondency that was so in evidence earlier had disappeared.

When she saw Lark standing in front of the glass etagère, dusting and rearranging the expensive collection of Royal Doulton china figurines, Candace tossed the racket aside and bounded over to hug her. Lark was surprised; Jonathan's daughter had never been demonstrative with her. But she hugged her back as Candace said, "Thank you, Lark. You made me feel a lot better. I wish you were my mother."

Lark was caught off guard by that, but she managed to compose herself and grin. "That's the nicest thing you could have said to me. I wish you were my daughter, but that would be a little bizarre since I'm only nine years older than you."

Candace was suddenly serious. "You could be my mother if you married my dad."

Lark's composure was totally done in. "I—I think you'd better let your father do the proposing around here. He may prefer to pick his own wife."

Candace giggled. "I've seen the way he looks at you. All he needs is a little push."

"No, Candace." Lark's tone was harsher than she'd intended, and she took a moment to soften it before she continued. "Your dad has no intention of marrying again, and you'd only embarrass him if you tried matchmaking."

Candace's expression changed to one of sadness. "Yeah, I guess he had a bellyful of Mom."

"Candace!" Lark had never heard the girl speak disrespectfully of anyone before, certainly not her mother.

"Well, it's true," she said. "Mom never thought of anyone but herself. She made Dad so miserable he finally left us, and then she had the nerve to blame *him*."

Lark couldn't let Candace make such judgmental statements unchallenged. "Honey," she said gently, "you can't possibly have all the facts. Don't you think you may be too hard on your mother?"

"No, I don't," she answered. "You're the one that doesn't know, Lark. I lived with her for fifteen years. I know all the times she left me with baby-sitters and was gone most of the night when Dad wasn't home. I know how she fought Dad for custody of Patty and me, then griped all the time because we were in her way. I was old enough when they were divorced that I could have chosen to live with Dad, but I couldn't because I knew my mother would never take proper care of Patty if I wasn't there to do it for her. She was too busy running around. Patty always came to *me* for attention, never Mom."

Candace turned away, and Lark could have cried for the girl. She put her arm around Candace's waist. "Oh, honey, I'm so sorry. Forgive me for speaking out of turn."

Candace nodded and Lark hugged her tighter. Now tha
they were on the subject, she might as well try to find ou
what Rob wanted to know. "Candace," she said, "have yo
heard from your mother since she left here? Do you know
where she is?"

Candace looked at her with surprise. "No, I haven't hear
from her, and I don't have any idea where she is. No on
does. She's being hateful to Dad again. She knows he'
worry about her."

"You worry about her too, don't you?" Lark said, an
her voice was laced with sympathy for the child.

"No. I ... well, maybe a little," Candace stammered de
fensively.

Lark's arms tightened around her. "Don't feel guilty
about your concern; it's a natural feeling. After all, Gisell
is your mother. You're not being disloyal to your father. H
doesn't want you to be bitter."

For a moment Candace yielded to the embrace, the
pulled away. "Yeah, you're right," she said. "I do worry
about her some. I don't want her to come back, but I wish
she'd let us know where she is and if she's all right."

She walked over to the chair and picked up her tennis
racket. "Is it okay if I go to the club with Maribeth? I told
her I'd pick her up."

Lark smiled. "Sure, but drive carefully."

Candace turned to look at her and grinned. "You sound
just like my dad," she said, and bounded out of the house.

Lark was torn between relief and despair. Candace would
be okay, and now she had all the information Rob had sent
her to get, but it also meant she would have to leave the
Nolan home as soon as possible. Her mission had just run
out.

That evening at dinner Jonathan told Candace and Patty that their grandparents, the Ulrics, had called that afternoon. They were back from their Alaska cruise and wanted to see their granddaughters the following day. Since he had no way of knowing that Lark already knew his ex-in-laws, he explained to her that they were Giselle's parents and were allowed to take the children on occasion for a day or two at a time.

Lark felt the stirrings of panic. Did the Ulrics know she was living in Jonathan's house as his housekeeper? They had left on their cruise before Rob had had a chance to tell them. Would they even recognize her if they saw her? Probably not. She'd more or less melted into the background that day, and they'd been distraught over their daughter's continued absence. Still, she'd have to get in touch with Rob as soon as possible and tell him to make sure his clients didn't blow her cover.

Candace was anything but enthusiastic, but she agreed to go with her grandparents. She was adamant on one point, however. "We won't stay more than one day. There's nothing to do over there, and Grandma's got all those fragile and expensive things sitting around. They fascinate Patty and she always wants to pick them up and play with them but if she breaks one Grandma has hysterics."

While Candace was doing the dishes and Jonathan was putting Patty to bed, Lark went into the den to call Rob. The phone was answered by a baby-sitter who said Rob and Melanie had gone to a party and weren't expected home until late. Lark didn't leave a message, but she made a mental note to contact Rob at his office first thing the next morning.

Later, when Candace had gone upstairs to wash her hair and indulge in one of her interminable phone conversations with Maribeth, Lark was sitting in the living room

watching a videotape of a detective show when Jonathan
wandered in. He stood watching in silence for a few minutes, then said, "I thought that was on earlier in the week."

Lark looked up at him and grinned. "It is, but I was busy
the other night and couldn't watch, so I taped it."

"You like police shows, do you?" He walked over and sat
on the sofa beside her.

"You bet. Never miss 'em. Now be quiet or we'll miss
some of the plot and never be able to catch up."

He chuckled and captured her hand in his as he settled
down to watch.

She tried to keep her mind on the show, but all her nerve
ends seemed centered in the hand that snuggled in his big
warm one.

When the show was over she picked up the remote control and switched the video player off and the television on.
"What do you want to watch now?" she asked.

Jonathan looked at his watch, then without letting go of
her hand picked up the *TV Guide*. "Let's see," he drawled,
"how about a mystery? I really go for private detectives."

Oh God, Lark thought, if only he remembers that when
he finds out he's under investigation.

"Lark, what's the matter?" Jonathan's anxious voice finally penetrated, and she realized she'd dropped the remote
control switch and messed up the television picture in the
process.

She hurriedly picked it up and adjusted the picture.
"Sorry, just klutzy I guess." She hurried on. "There's an
old movie on one of the local stations that I wanted to see."

She flipped the stations until a title appeared on the
screen: *Jane Eyre* starring Joan Fontaine and Orson Welles.

Jonathan groaned dramatically. "Jeez, do we have to sit
through that mushy stuff?" he teased.

Lark was regaining her composure. "Stop complaining and enjoy," she said, trying not to giggle. "You could stand a little culture. This is a classic."

"You're going to be disappointed," he predicted gleefully. "There aren't even any passionate love scenes."

"Of course not," she said with just the right amount of virtue. "Mr. Rochester had a mad wife in the attic."

Jonathan reached for her then, and pulled her into the circle of his arms so that she fitted comfortably with her back against his chest. "Maybe he was wrong," Jonathan said thoughtfully, "to let an impossible marriage come between him and the one woman who could have made him happy."

Lark knew that he wasn't thinking only of Edward Rochester, but for once she had the good sense not to comment. Instead she settled against him, and in the dim light of the room they watched the movie.

For a while they were engrossed in the ill-fated romance unfolding on the screen, but after a time Lark was aware that Jonathan's hand had moved upward to just below her breast, its fullness resting against his thumb and wrist. She tried to ignore it, but her heart beat had speeded up and she was sure he could feel it.

She made a determined effort to concentrate on the movie, but when he moved again, this time to cup the firm round flesh, she shivered and he lowered his head to trail light kisses down the side of her sensitive neck. She moaned and put her hand over his as his fingers gently stroked her.

"Jonathan." It was a cross between a sigh and a protest.

"Do you always wear a bra?" he whispered against her ear.

"Usually," she said, before his lips and his fingers made her forget the question. "Jonathan, you shouldn't ... You said ..."

"I talk too much," he murmured. "I won't do anything you don't want me to, but don't stop me yet. I've ached to touch you like this again ever since that day in the forest. I didn't think it could feel as good as I remembered, but it does."

She couldn't have stopped him, any more than he could stop himself.

When he began to unbutton her plum silk blouse, she shifted to make it easier for him, and when he slipped it off her shoulders she leaned forward so he could unhook the constricting bra and remove it, too. He turned her then so she was lying across his lap, and his gaze roamed over her nude shoulders and breasts. "You're exquisite," he said, and bent to press his face against her creamy skin.

She loved the softness of his beard when it brushed her in such an intimate place, and she threaded her fingers through his hair and held him to her. He moved his head and took her nipple in his mouth, sending shock waves to the core of her womanhood. She clenched fistfuls of his hair as his tongue made slow circles around her hard, rosy tip, then moved to the other breast where he repeated the sweet torture.

She wanted to pleasure him as he was pleasuring her, and her hands roamed over his shoulders and back, but his clothes were in the way. She wanted to feel his bareness as he was feeling hers. She inched his loose shirt away from his slacks and slid her hands under it. He shivered as her palms made contact, and he paused long enough to pull the shirt over his head.

Again he gathered her to him, and her throbbing breasts pressed eagerly against the rough dark hair of his chest. "Oh, Lark, Lark," he groaned, and nibbled at her lower lip before capturing her mouth with his own.

Lark was lost to everything but Jonathan—his lips possessing hers; his hands caressing her breasts, her derriere; the hot bare flesh and muscle of his back under her searching touch. He broke the kiss just long enough for them to breathe, then once more plundered her with his impatient tongue.

They were too immersed in their runaway passion to be aware of anything else until suddenly a shrill little voice not more than two feet away shattered their preoccupation. "Daddy, I had a bad dream!" It was Patty, standing beside the sofa barefoot and in her pajamas.

They jumped and pulled away from each other so quickly that Lark was thrown off balance and clutched at the back of the couch to keep from falling off. She had the presence of mind to stay in that position, with her bare back to the child. She buried her flushed face in the cushion until Jonathan got to his feet, swung his daughter into his arms and hurried out to the hall, crooning soothing words to the frightened little girl.

Lark put on her blouse and buttoned it with fingers that had become all thumbs. She switched off the television and the dim lamp, and stood silently in the dark until she was sure Jonathan and Patty had gone up the stairs. Then she ran down the hall to the bathroom and locked the door.

Her intention was to take a shower, but her legs were shaking so, that she had to sit down on the side of the bathtub. She felt overwhelmed with shame. How could she and Jonathan have gotten so carried away as to make love in the open living room with a light on and no thought of the children who might wander in?

She knew this had never happened to Jonathan before. He wouldn't take a woman home to spend the night when his children were there. His concern for his daughters' innocence was one of the reasons he'd refused to hire Lark initially.

She shuddered and put her face in her hands. Just this morning she'd lectured Candace about not leading men on, and then she'd been caught in the act of doing that very thing herself. And with the girl's own father! Thank God it was Patty who had interrupted them instead of Candace.

A knock on the door startled Lark. "Lark, are you all right? Let me in." It was Jonathan.

"I'm okay," she said, trying to keep her voice from shaking.

"Open the door, honey," he said, and rattled the knob. "I want to talk to you."

She wrapped her arms around herself and sat huddled on the tub. "Not tonight, Jonathan. I—I'm just getting ready to take a shower."

For a moment there was silence, then he said wearily. "All right, but we'll talk tomorrow morning before I leave for the office."

The next morning there was no chance for privacy. Both Candace and Patty were up early and had breakfast with Jonathan and Lark so they could be ready to go when their grandparents came to get them. Nor did Lark have a chance to call Rob again, but since she wasn't expecting the Ulrics to arrive until late morning, she wasn't too anxious. She'd wait until Jonathan left for work.

But Jonathan got a long-distance telephone call just as he was preparing to leave, and it went on and on while Lark nervously watched the clock. She had to let Rob know the Ulrics were coming so he could warn them that she was the new housekeeper.

Finally Jonathan came out of the den with his briefcase. He kissed Candace and Patty goodbye and told them to behave themselves at their grandparents' home, then took Lark's arm and ushered her into the kitchen. When the door closed behind them he put his arm around her and pulled her close. "Goodbye, love, and please, don't worry about last night. Everything's going to be all right, I promise. I'll tell you about it tonight."

He kissed her quick and hard, then disappeared out the door that led to the garage.

Lark stood there dazed. What had he meant by that remark? How could everything be all right? He didn't seem very upset about being caught in a compromising situation with her. He seemed cheerful, happy, even a little relieved. Was it possible he'd changed his mind about not becoming involved with her? Surely not. He'd been definite. But still . . .

She snapped back to reality, determined not to dream impossible dreams, and headed for the den where she could use the phone in private. As she passed the living room Candace called out, asking her to come in. Lark entered the room she'd left so hastily the night before, and found Candace struggling to put shoes on Patty, who was resisting vigorously. "No, don't want shoes," the child whined. "Go barefooten."

Lark intervened just as the doorbell rang, and Candace handed her the shoes and started toward the entryway. "I'll get it. It's probably Nancy Scottsworth from next door. She promised to save yesterday's *San Francisco Chronicle* for me."

Lark turned her attention to Patty and ignored the voices in the doorway until she realized they were coming closer. She stood and turned around as Patty shouted, "Grandma," and ran to throw herself into the outstretched arms of Alice Ulric, while Frederik stood behind her, waiting his turn.

Lark and Alice saw each other at the same time, and Alice's smile turned to an expression of amazement. "Why, Miss Carlisle, Lark, what are you doing here?" she asked as she hugged Patty and handed her to an equally amazed Frederik. "Don't tell me your brother planted you here as a housekeeper? He said that was the best way to investigate Jonathan, but I understood you were only visit—"

Her mouth snapped shut as she belatedly realized that Candace was standing by Lark, hearing every word of her unfortunate revelation.

The blood drained from Lark's face and she felt sick. For a moment they were all shocked into a stunned silence that was finally broken by an agonizingly familiar male voice.

"Yes, *Miss Carlisle*," Jonathan said from the wide arch entrance to the room. "I think we'd all be interested to hear just what in hell you *are* doing here."

His tone was as cold and hard as the expression on his face.

Chapter Nine

Lark couldn't have spoken if her life had depended on it. Her vocal cords were paralyzed, as was the rest of her. She could only stare at the man who just minutes before had been so warm and loving with her. Now he stood stiff and unbending, his hands clenched at his sides, his brown eyes frozen with disgust and recrimination.

It was like a movie that had been stopped in the middle of a scene: Alice Ulric cut off in midsentence; her husband, Frederik, blinking in confusion as he held his small grand-daughter; and Candace, her eyes wide with disbelief.

It was Patty who broke the awful silence. Somehow sensing that her father was upset, she tried to wiggle free of her grandfather, crying, "Down. I want my daddy."

Frederik stood her on the floor, and she ran to Jonathan and wrapped her arms around his leg. The movement brought them all back to life, and Jonathan reached down and picked up his daughter.

Alice was the first to find her voice. "Jonathan, I didn't know you were here." There was fear beneath her bluster.

"Obviously not," Jonathan replied in that frosty tone.

His glance swung back to Lark. "I gather you've teamed with my ex-in-laws in another attempt to take my children away from me."

His words were like a jab in the stomach, and nausea twisted her insides and brought beads of perspiration to her forehead. "No! Oh no," she said, and swallowed the bile that rose to her throat. "You don't understand."

Jonathan cradled Patty in his arms. "Then suppose you tell me." He was looking at her with an expression reserved for things rather than people.

Before Lark could answer, Alice broke in. "Don't be silly, Jonathan," she said, her voice pitched high in her nervousness. "Rob Carlisle introduced Lark to us at a social gathering. She'd recently arrived in town, and we mentioned that you were looking for a housekeeper. I didn't know she'd applied for the job; that's why I was surprised to see her."

Lark wanted to scream at the woman to be quiet, she was only making things worse.

It was Jonathan who silenced her. "Shut up, Alice. I want to hear it from Lark." He shifted his gaze. "Now you tell me what's going on around here." It wasn't a request, it was a command.

She sank down on the couch, no longer able to stand on her trembling legs. "My name is Lark Carlisle Bancroft, but I dropped the Bancroft four years ago when I divorced Wayne. I'm Rob Carlisle's younger sister, and I was visiting him when..."

She shook her head and put her hand to her stomach in an effort to soothe the rolling nausea that threatened to erupt any minute.

If Jonathan was aware of her distress, he gave no indication. "When what? Come on, I want the whole story."

Again Alice spoke up. "You don't have to tell him a thing, Lark." She walked over and sat on the couch beside Lark. "Don't let him browbeat you into saying things that aren't true."

Jonathan glared at Alice. "If you don't stop interrupting, I'm going to put you out, even if I have to do it forcibly."

"Now, see here..." Frederik finally joined the conversation.

"No, *you* see here." Jonathan's tone would have stopped a hurricane. "I've had all I'm going to take from you people. You've been mucking up my life for almost twenty years, and I've finally reached the end of my endurance. No more. When you leave here you'll be barred from ever entering my house again, and if you want to stay now to hear what Lark has to say you'll sit quietly and not speak unless you're spoken to."

Both Alice and Frederik paled even more, and Frederik stumbled to a chair and seated himself.

Jonathan's gaze found his elder daughter, and he beckoned to her. "Candace. Come here, sweetheart."

There were tears in her eyes as she moved across the room toward him. Jonathan reached out his empty arm and pulled her to his side. "I think you'd better take Patty and go upstairs. There's no need for you to hear all this."

Candace shook her head and pressed closer to her father. "No, Daddy, I'm not going to leave you."

For a second the mask that was his face crumbled and Lark caught a glimpse of the searing pain he was concealing, but it disappeared even as he lowered his head to kiss the top of his daughter's head. When he looked up again the shield was securely in place.

His gaze returned to Lark, freezing her with its ice. "You were saying?"

She was too shaken to plan what she was going to say; she just started at the beginning and told him everything. How she had been on her way to Rob's office the morning she collided with Jonathan and hurt her hand; the meeting with the Ulrics and their insistence that Rob investigate Jonathan; how she had begged Rob to let her do the investigating; and her shock at finding that Jonathan was the same man she'd bumped into.

She didn't let anything personal creep into her narrative. If she had she'd have broken down completely. Instead she told it as quickly and unemotionally as she could. Now and then a sob escaped her tight control, but she finally concluded by admitting that she'd carefully searched the house and questioned his neighbors and friends.

When it was over she felt drained and exhausted. There was so much more she wanted to say. She wanted to tell him that Rob had never doubted his innocence, but had only taken on the investigation to keep the Ulrics from going to a less scrupulous agency. She wanted to assure him that she'd been more concerned with taking care of him and his daughters than with the investigation, and that she'd taken special care not to cause suspicion or to damage his reputation in any way with her questions. She wanted to go to him and put her arms around him and tell him she loved him, that she had never believed he had anything to do with his wife's disappearance.

She wanted to tell him all these things, but knew he wasn't in the mood to hear them. She couldn't embarrass him by talking about their personal relationship in front of his daughters and their grandparents. Besides, it didn't matter. He'd never believe her. He'd think she was just trying to appeal to the tender feelings he'd had for her—and which she had now killed for all time.

Lark slumped against the back of the sofa and covered her eyes with the palms of her hands. Her stomach was still in an uproar, and she felt dizzy.

Jonathan had been standing all this time, holding Patty in one arm and pressing Candace to him with the other. Now he spoke again to Candace. "Honey, I want you to take Patty and go upstairs. I have some unpleasant things to say and I don't want you to hear them."

Lark uncovered her eyes as Candace started to protest, but he hurried on. "We'll talk later, I promise. I'm not trying to keep anything from you, but I'd rather we talked when we can be alone together. Right now you can help me most by taking Patty up to her room."

Candace put her arms around her father and kissed him, then took her little sister from him and left the room.

Jonathan still didn't sit down, but stood facing the others. He looked ill, but even so there was an aura of strength about him that was chilling. Lark had never seen this side of him. She knew only the soft-spoken man who was gentle and loving with his daughters and with her; who had married a woman he didn't love because it was his duty; who had stayed with his wife for years because she was his responsibility.

For the first time she was seeing the hard powerful core of him. The tough businessman who fought for what was his and gave no quarter.

His face remained cold, shuttered, but his eyes blazed with rage as he turned toward the Ulrics. "I hadn't intended for you to know this," he said, and the tender tone he'd used with Candace was replaced with a biting intensity. "I thought it would serve no useful purpose and would only hurt you, but I was wrong. My biggest mistake was not taking Giselle and moving as far away from you as we could get when we were first married. But she didn't want to leave Eureka, and I was still in college, so we stayed. We might have had a chance at happiness if she'd had to grow up, but you never allowed that. You made it so easy for her to come to you if she wanted something I wouldn't give her, or for sympathy and absolution after we'd had a quarrel.''

Alice straightened with righteous indignation and started to say something, but Jonathan quelled her with a look. ''I put up with it as long as I could, but eventually, for the sake of my own sanity, I had to leave her. I didn't anticipate any problem in getting custody of the children. She'd never wanted either of them and did nothing but complain about having to take care of them.''

This time Alice wouldn't be squelched. ''That's not true,'' she said indignantly. ''Giselle adored her daughters.''

''Oh knock it off, Alice,'' Jonathan grated. ''You never made any effort to really know Giselle. You only saw what you wanted to see, and heard what she wanted to tell you. You couldn't bear to think that your precious little girl might not be the perfect angel you wanted her to be.''

He started pacing. ''I was unprepared when she fought my petition for custody the first time and I lost, but when I realized she wasn't taking proper care of the children I tried again. This time I was better prepared, but still I was no match for Giselle. She was beautiful, a good actress, and an accomplished liar. It was beginning to look as if I would lose again, when I was presented with indisputable evidence that would not only prove her an unfit mother, but could also send her to jail.''

Both of the Ulrics gasped, and this time it was Frederik who protested. ''Now that's enough, Jonathan. I'll not sit here and listen to you malign my daughter!'' He was on his feet and sputtering with indignation.

"You'd damn well better or I'll have a warrant issued for her arrest." Jonathan didn't raise his voice, but still it carried to the far corners of the room.

Lark sat up, totally alert now. Had Giselle broken the law? If so, how? What else had she done to torment Jonathan? And where was she?

Frederik's bluster collapsed like a pierced balloon, and he sat down again, looking older than he had a few minutes before.

Jonathan ran his hand through his hair and again started to pace. "Without naming names or places," he began, "I learned that Giselle was working with a narcotics dealer to supply cocaine to some of her avant-garde friends in order to supplement the support I was paying her."

This time both of the Ulrics rose. "That's not true," they shouted in unison.

"My baby would never do such a thing," Alice continued. "She wouldn't take drugs."

"You're right about that," Jonathan said. "She wasn't taking cocaine, she was selling it. She was as greedy as ever. Even with all the money I was paying her she wanted more, but she sure as hell wasn't prepared to be arrested. When I confronted her with the evidence and threatened to go to the police if she didn't give me full and undisputed custody of our daughters until they turned eighteen, she couldn't sign the agreement quickly enough."

"I knew it," Alice screamed. "You blackmailed her."

"Damn right I did," Jonathan growled. "I'd have done anything to get my daughters away from her influence. The last thing I wanted was to have them grow up like their mother. On the other hand, I preferred that they be spared the knowledge that she had been dealing in drugs."

Lark sat on the edge of the couch. So this is what Jonathan meant when he said he'd quarreled with Giselle before she left. Did he also send her away?

The question was given voice by Frederik. "Where is Giselle?" he asked. "What did you do with her? Apparently we were right all along. You did have something to do with her disappearance."

Jonathan shook his head. "You're wrong. All I demanded was custody of the children, and her promise to stay out of the drug business. Neither of us said anything about her leaving the area. I have no idea where she is. Obviously it's her way of getting back at me for daring to get the upper hand. I never had to use the agreement she signed. I got custody by default."

There was an uneasy silence that was broken by Alice. "I don't believe a word you've said," she exclaimed, but the conviction was gone from her tone. "Giselle isn't like that. She'd never have anything to do with drugs."

Jonathan shrugged. "That's your prerogative, but if you give me any more trouble, I'll turn my evidence over to the police. I can guarantee they'll find her and arrest her."

Alice began to cry, and Frederik walked over to her. "We'll go now," he said in a voice that sounded very old. "Come, my dear."

As they walked wearily toward the entryway, Jonathan spoke. "I don't want you to come here, or to try to contact my daughters in any way. You're no longer a part of my family."

Lark shuddered. Jonathan had almost inexhaustible patience but there was a limit, and once that limit was reached he could be ruthless and unforgiving. She almost felt sorry for the Ulrics.

As soon as the door shut behind them, Jonathan turned to confront Lark. He stood several feet from the couch where she sat huddled with her arms across her midsection. She looked small, and young, and shattered, almost as if she had been wrongly accused.

He closed his eyes to shut her out. Dear God, what was wrong with him? Was he fated to go through life always falling in love with the wrong woman? Well, he wouldn't have to worry about it ever happening again. It would be a cold day in hell before he'd let his emotions get involved with another female. He'd said that once before, but then Lark came along with her warmth and her sweetness and charmed him into letting down his guard. He'd been the perfect patsy. He'd given her total access to his home, his children, and his friends. Worse yet, he'd given her his love. The love he'd thought had been destroyed by Giselle.

He opened his eyes. This time he'd learned his lesson. Never again would he let a woman put him through the torment he was experiencing now. All he had to do was send Lark away and the pain would begin to recede.

"Well, Lark, you must have been doing pretty well financially, drawing two salaries," he said in a voice laced with sarcasm. "One from Rob Carlisle and one from me. Or do you work for Rob for free, just for the fun of it? Oh, yes, and I believe you mentioned something about needing the experience for when you join the police force. You'll be one hell of a good police officer, but I have to admit I feel a little sorry for the male criminals in Phoenix. Is there anything you *wouldn't* do to get information?"

Lark cringed. How could she persuade him to listen to her side of this? She couldn't look at him; didn't want to see the loathing in his eyes. "I don't blame you for hating me, Jonathan, but please let me explain." She spoke barely above a whisper. "I never meant to harm you."

"Oh, that's good to hear. I'll remind myself of that when the shock wears off and I feel the full force of the knife you shoved in my back. When I have to deal with the pain of having been made a fool of.''

She shook her head. "No. I'm the fool. I thought I could prove you were innocent of the Ulrics' charges and you'd never have to know about the investigation. Rob only took on this case so they wouldn't go to someone else who might embarrass you or make things difficult.''

Jonathan again started to pace. "That was real friendly of him. I suppose you think things aren't difficult now? That I'm not as humiliated as it's possible to be?''

He strode angrily to the sofa and gripped her upper arms, pulling her up. "Look at me, dammit!" The sarcasm had been replaced with rage. "At least have the decency to look me in the face when you lie to me.''

She could feel the heat radiating from his body, and his hands were clamped painfully on her shoulders as he shook her.

"Please, Jonathan, I'm not lying," she shouted, knowing that was the only way she could hope to get through to him. "When I agreed to take this job I didn't know who you were. That first day, when I realized that Jonathan Nolan was the man who'd been so gentle and caring with me when I hurt my hand, I wanted to turn and run. I was almost relieved when you refused to hire me, and when you called and asked me to come back I came because you and the girls needed my help.''

"You're a regular little ministering angel, aren't you?" he sneered. "I suppose you're going to tell me that gossiping about me with my neighbors and snooping through my personal things was all for my own good.''

"I understand how you feel, but no one knew what I was doing. I was careful not to arouse suspicion, and I didn't see anything in your personal items I wouldn't have run across normally in the course of my housekeeping duties.''

He dropped his hands to his sides and turned away. "But I did have a secret. What if I'd carelessly left the evidence of Giselle's drug dealing in a desk drawer? Would you have gone to Rob and the Ulrics with that? Would you have let the whole town know about it before I'd had a chance to prepare Candace? Don't tell me it was a harmless pastime."

Lark's throat was filled and her eyes burned with unshed tears. She wished she could cry, but for some reason that release was denied her. Sobs choked her, and moisture dimmed her vision, but neither would break through. "I don't know what I would have done, and I'm not trying to justify my actions, but if I hadn't done it someone else would have. At least I would have protected you."

He swung around to glare at her. "Protected me! My God, I can do without your brand of protection. You sure as hell weren't protecting me last night here on the couch. If Patty hadn't interrupted us you'd have let me make love to you, wouldn't you?"

The time for pretense was long past. "Yes," she said softly.

His shoulders slumped, and he threaded his fingers through his hair. "You know what that makes you, don't you?"

"Yes," she said quietly. "It makes me a woman in love who could no longer resist her feelings. My very first mistake was falling in love with you."

Once again, for just a second, his composure cracked and she saw the naked anguish behind it, but then it was gone. "Love!" He spat out the word as if it had a foul taste. "You don't know what love is all about. You confuse it with sex and use it to get what you want from a man. You're just like Giselle, only not as honest. At least when she cuddled up to me, we both knew why and what we would get out of it. She got her own way, and I got my needs taken care of.''

Lark winced and clapped her hands to her ears. She didn't want to hear about his lovemaking with his ex-wife. She couldn't bear to think of another woman lying nude in his arms, exciting him to madness. "Don't. Oh please, don't," she pleaded. "I'm not like that. I wanted you. I still want you, love you, need you. Oh, darling. I didn't mean to hurt you so.''

With breathtaking suddenness his arms encircled her, hauling her roughly against him in an imprisoning embrace. "So you want me, do you?'' he growled. "Well, honey, I'm not one to refuse such an impassioned proposition. I wouldn't want you to go away unsatisfied.''

His mouth ground into hers, and one hand held the back of her head while the other one pushed her lower body into his. It was a violent, punishing embrace that had nothing to do with love, or even wanting. She couldn't move or protest as his tongue plundered and his teeth bit into her soft flesh.

For the first time she knew fear in a man's arms, and she pummeled him with her fists, but he seemed not to notice. The strength of his grasp was suffocating, and she couldn't breathe. What on earth had she unleashed in him? This wasn't Jonathan. Jonathan wouldn't— As quickly as he had grabbed her he released her and flung her aside so that she landed in a sprawl on the couch. He stood over her and his eyes were ablaze, not with passion but with fury. "You little—" The name he wanted to call her was ancient and ugly. "It's too bad my daughters are in the house. You owe me, and I'd take great pleasure in collecting. Now get up and start packing. I'm going upstairs and talk to Candace, try to undo some of the damage you've done to my children. I'll be up there for an hour, and when I come back down I want you and everything that belongs to you out of my house. If I ever see you again, I won't be responsible for what happens."

He straightened up and stalked out of the room, leaving Lark gasping for breath and trembling with shock and anguish.

The next few days were a haze of misery for Lark. She remembered packing in silence and leaving the Nolan home without seeing Jonathan or the girls again. She'd managed not to go through any red lights or stop signs, and arrived at Rob's house safely, then collapsed in Melanie's arms when the storm of weeping finally broke loose and shook her with its violence.

The rest of the time was a blur. She couldn't eat, and she couldn't sleep, and although she tried to make conversation when people spoke to her, she had no idea what she said. Rob and Melanie looked worried, and conferred in whispers, and her little nephews kept their distance.

She knew she was a source of concern to her family, but she couldn't do anything about it. Even when her marriage broke up she hadn't been this shattered, and she marveled at the strength of the love she felt for a man she'd known less than a month. If it weren't for the guilt she might have fared better, but knowing that she had deliberately set out to deceive Jonathan, that she'd continued to deceive him even when she knew she was falling in love with him, gnawed at her soul. She'd coolly gone about setting him up for the agony he'd suffered when he found out who she was and what she'd done.

She couldn't blame him for not believing a word she said. She'd feel the same way if their roles were reversed. She'd killed any chance of including Jonathan and his daughters

in her life, even as friends, and she had no one but herself
to blame.

On Saturday, Rob sent Melanie and the boys to a mati-
nee movie, then took Lark into the family room and seated
them both on the sofa. "Lark, this can't go on," he said
carefully. "You're losing weight, and you act like a zom-
bie. If you don't snap out of it you're going to have a
breakdown."

She looked into her brother's hazel eyes and saw the
worry mirrored there. "I'm sorry, Rob," she said, and she
was. She didn't want to cause him concern. "I just don't
seem to be able to function." Her eyes filled with tears she
hadn't been able to turn off once they'd started. "Oh Rob,
I hurt so."

Rob reached out and took her in his arms. "I know, baby,
I know," he crooned softly, "and I feel so damned guilty. I
should never have let you take on that job. I knew you didn't
have the experience to handle it, but it seemed like such a
simple thing. I never expected you to fall in love with the
man."

Lark rubbed her wet cheek in Rob's shoulder. "Don't
blame yourself, Rob. It's not your fault. I was the hot-shot
graduate with a brand-new degree in criminal justice. I was
going to dazzle everyone with my brilliance, and make
brownie points for myself with police departments every-
where." She rubbed her other cheek with her fist. "You
should have sent me back home and told me to grow up."

He patted her gently on the back. "We both should have
done things differently, but we didn't, so it's time to stop
blaming ourselves and get on with trying to repair the damage. I haven't told you this before, but I went to see Jon."

Lark stiffened. "You did? When? How is he? How are
Candace and Patty? Do they hate me too?"

"Hey now, hold on." He settled her head back on his shoulder. "When we finally got you calmed down on Tuesday, I phoned the Nolan residence, but no one answered. I decided it would be a good idea to let Jon cool off a little anyway, so I waited until the next morning and phoned his office. His secretary gave me an appointment, but then called back later to cancel it and said she wasn't sure when he'd be available to see me. Obviously he had no intention of talking to me, so that night after dinner I went to the house unannounced."

A sob shook Lark. "Was he there? Did you see him? Oh, Rob, is he all right?"

"He was there and I saw him, and he looked like hell, but no worse than you do. At first he wasn't going to let me in, threatened to sue and that sort of thing."

"Oh no!"

"It's all right, he was just blowing off steam. He finally let me in and even gave me a drink while we talked. I tried to explain what had happened, why we took the case, but he wasn't having any of it. I can't say that I blame him. Giselle was a witch to live with, but he'd finally found a little peace of mind with his children and we went and stirred it all up again. I still think I was right to take the case, but it ruined a budding friendship that I valued. There's no chance that he'll ever forgive me."

Lark sighed. "Or me. I could have made him happy. I know I could, and Candace was even talking about how she'd like me for a mother." She stifled another sob. "How is Candace? Have they found another housekeeper?"

"I don't know. I didn't see either of the girls or a housekeeper, and I didn't dare question Jon about anything. I'd guess that he hasn't replaced you yet. The house had sort of a cluttered look."

Rob sat Lark up and looked at her. "Now, let's get back to you. If you don't get a hold of yourself and start eating and sleeping you're going to be sick. I know you're not doing it deliberately, but maybe it would help to think of Dad. He's had two heart attacks. You don't want him to see you like this. You know how protective he is of his only daughter."

Lark felt ashamed of her self-pitying moping. "You're right," she said, and pushed her shoulder-length hair out of her eyes. "I don't want to worry Dad, and I don't want to be such a drag on you and Melanie. I'll make an effort to shape up, I promise."

He pulled her back in his arms and hugged her. "That's my independent little sister," he said with a grin. "Let Melanie fatten you up some. She knows all about nutrition and all that jazz." The grin disappeared before he spoke again. "And, honey, much as we love having you here, I think you'd better give some thought to going back to Phoenix. You aren't going to get over this as long as you stay in Eureka. You'll always be looking for Jonathan Nolan around every corner."

"I know," she said sadly. "I've been thinking the same thing. I'll leave just as soon as I start looking a little better. If Dad could see me now he'd have a third coronary."

Lark began forcing herself to eat and to take an interest in what was going on around her. She found that the high-energy meals Melanie fed her family made her feel better. Not happier, but a little less depressed, and by Tuesday she was making plans to return to Phoenix at the end of the week. She took her car in for a tune-up, and called her parents to tell them she was coming.

On Thursday she had started packing, intending to leave early the next morning, when she heard a car drive into the driveway, and a minute later the back door that led to the kitchen slammed as someone came in. She heard Melanie talking to somebody, but Lark's attention remained on her packing until heavy footsteps came bounding up the stairs and Rob appeared in her open doorway.

She blinked with surprise. "Rob, what are you doing home at this time of day? It's not even noon yet."

He grinned and looked inordinately pleased. "I've got some news for you, and it wouldn't wait. Lark, we've found Giselle Nolan."

The dress she was folding dropped out of her hands. "Oh my God! Is she all right?" Her knees gave way and she dropped down on the side of the bed.

"She's fine," Rob chortled, "and working in a gambling casino in Las Vegas. She's remarried and uses her husband's last name. That's why we've had such a time finding her."

"Married!" Lark's mind seemed to have suspended operation. "But who? Why did she just disappear?" She was struggling to make sense of what she'd heard, when the most important question of all finally surfaced. "Have you told Jonathan?"

Rob took her arm and pulled her up. "Not yet. Come on downstairs so I can tell you and Melanie about it at the same time."

In the kitchen they sat around the table with mugs of coffee while Rob told his story. "As you already know, we had reason to believe Giselle had gone to Las Vegas, but we couldn't find her. We searched Reno, Carson City and Lake Tahoe, too, but couldn't turn her up anywhere. We finally decided to concentrate on her first name—it's not all that common. We checked out everyone we could find named Giselle working in casinos and finally came up with Giselle Alvarez.

"Alvarez?" Lark and Melanie chorused.

Rob chuckled. "Her husband's the big, tough, chauvin-istic type who calls all the shots and doesn't take any non-sense. He cracks the whip, and she jumps, and according to my operative they're madly in love. Can you beat it? Ap-parently what she needed was someone to take command and keep her in line."

Lark took a long swallow of her coffee. "The woman must be out of her mind to prefer any man over Jona-than," she observed. "But what about her children, and her parents? Did she say why she hasn't contacted them?"

Rob shrugged. "She wouldn't talk about her past life. In fact, my operative said she was pretty upset about being found. My guess is that Jon scared the hell out of her when he threatened to have her arrested on drug charges and she just took off. She's not very maternal, and she knew Jon would take better care of the kids than she could. It's really none of our business now. If he wants to question her, I'll tell him where he can find her."

"So you haven't told him yet. What about the Ulrics?"

"So far I haven't told anyone but you. Ordinarily the Ulrics are the only ones I'd report to, but since I'm offi-cially off the case now, I'm not bound by that restriction."

Lark felt an almost debilitating sense of relief. Giselle had been found not only safe but happy. There was no longer a cloud over Jonathan's integrity. Maybe now he could really have the peace of mind that had been denied him for so long. At least the investigation had done that much. Maybe some day he could forgive Lark for her part in it.

She jumped when Rob touched her arm. "Hey, little sis-ter, you're not paying attention," he said, and she realized she'd been deep in thought.

"I'm sorry," she said apologetically, "what were you saying?"

He was suddenly serious. "I said I think you should be the one to tell Jon that we've found Giselle."

Lark's mouth dropped open. "You're kidding."

"Honey, that's one thing I wouldn't kid about. I want you to go to Jon and give him the report."

A flicker of hope stirred within her. "But he'd never see me. He distinctly told me that he never wanted to see me again."

"Then do the same thing I did. Try to make an appointment, and if he refuses then go to his house. You deserve a chance to put things right. At least give it a try."

The hope grew, and with it a sense of excitement. If she could see him again, talk to him, give him the information he needed about his ex-wife, maybe he'd at least feel more kindly toward her. She didn't expect his forgiveness, but was it too much to wish for a little understanding?

"All right, Rob," she said. "I will. Do you have the phone number for his office?"

Rob produced the number and Lark dialed it with fingers that trembled. Even if she could only hear his voice it would help.

The ring was answered by his secretary, and Lark gave her name and said she'd like to make an appointment to see Mr. Nolan about a personal matter.

"I'm sorry, Ms. Carlisle, but Mr. Nolan isn't in the office today."

Lark's hopes plummeted. "Oh. Is there any way I can get in touch with him? It's really awfully important."

The secretary hesitated. "I don't know when he'll be back in the office," she finally said. "His two daughters are ill, and he's at home with them."

A knot of fear formed in Lark's stomach. "Candace and Patty ill? Is it serious?"

"I'm afraid so," the woman confirmed. "He's making arrangements to have the older one admitted to a hospital."

"Oh no!" Lark banged the phone down and turned toward the kitchen. "I'm going to Jonathan. There's something wrong with the girls," she called to a startled Rob and Melanie as she grabbed her purse and flew out the door.

Chapter Ten

For once Lark didn't take any wrong turns or misread street signs, and she got to the Nolan residence in record time. She brought the car to a screeching halt at the curb and jumped out. She was halfway up the walk when the big golden retriever, Blazer, came around the side of the house and loped toward her, a gleam of recognition on his happy face.

"Hi, Blazer," she cried, and wrapped her arms around the shaggy blond dog as he jumped up on her, nearly knocking her down. "You're glad to see me, aren't you? It's nice that somebody in the family is. Is your daddy home?"

The animal barked joyfully and licked her face as she tried to fight him off. "Down, boy," she ordered. "Good grief, it's like being greeted by a pony. Stay down, now, and walk along beside me."

The well-trained but exuberant pet obeyed but licked her hand all the way to the front door. Lark was thankful for the distraction; it kept her too occupied to worry about the reception she would get from Blazer's master. It wasn't until she'd rung the doorbell that her heart began to pound and sweat broke out on her forehead.

The dog barked impatiently when the bell wasn't immediately answered, and Lark had bent down to quiet him when the door opened. Her gaze traveled up gray slacks and a blue shirt to Jonathan's drawn face. He looked incredibly tired and worried.

For a moment they just stood looking at each other while Blazer sat innocently at Lark's feet with his tongue hanging out and his tail wagging against the cement porch. Jonathan was the first to speak. "Go away, Lark," he said. "I can't cope with you right now." He moved to close the door, and Lark put her hand out to stop him.

"No, please. I—I just heard that Candace and Patty are ill. I know you don't want me here, but I had to come. How are they, Jonathan? What's the matter with them?" Her voice broke, and she pressed her lips together to keep them from trembling.

Jonathan hesitated a moment, then recognized her genuine concern. "They have chicken pox," he said without moving away from the door. "They're both pretty sick, but I'm really worried about Candace. Her temperature is high, and she's restless and miserable."

Lark remembered when she had chicken pox at age six. She'd been hot, and sick, and she'd itched. Her mother had been almost continuously at her bedside day and night.

"Do you have help? A—a housekeeper?"

She saw him stiffen. "No" was all he said.

"But you can't take care of them by yourself." She knew immediately that that was the wrong thing to say.

Again he started to shut the door. "I'm getting along fine," he grated. "Now, if you'll excuse me—"

"No, Jonathan, please don't shut me out," she cried. "I've had the chicken pox. Let me help."

His mouth twisted in a grimace. "I don't need you," he said coldly.

"I know." Lark's voice was little more than a whisper. She cleared her throat and tried again. "But you need someone, and apparently I'm the only one available. If you don't let me share some of the nursing duties you're going to be sick, too. Then who'll take care of the girls?"

He slumped against the doorjamb and closed his eyes. She wanted so badly to put her arms around him, to soothe him and make everything better, to invite him to sleep with his head resting between her breasts as he had the night he came home from China.

Instead she pleaded softly, "Let me try to make up for some of the anguish I've cost you. I'll take good care of your daughters. I love them too."

He opened his eyes, but then turned away from her. "Come in" was all he said before he walked away and left her to close the door.

It was immediately apparent that Jonathan was unable to keep up with the demands of two sick children and a twelve-room house. The place was a mess. Lark stopped at the foot of the stairway. "Is it all right if I go up and see the girls?" she asked.

He turned and started up the steps. "Come on, I'll go with you. Candace may not want you here. She was awfully upset when she found out you'd been lying to her."

Lark caught her breath. "I didn't lie to her. Not about anything important. I lied to you about my background, and only as much as was necessary to get you to hire me."

They'd reached the top landing, and he turned to look at her. "Don't nitpick, Lark," he said sharply. "I'm having enough trouble coping with my sick daughters. I have neither the time nor the patience to wade through semantic booby traps."

He swung around and led her into Candace's room. The blinds were pulled and the room was dim and stuffy, the air fetid. There were soiled clothes and towels lying around; glasses partially filled with liquids vied for space on the bedside table with medicine bottles and sticky spoons.

Candace lay in the tousled bed that looked as if she had been thrashing about in it all night. The sheet and blanket were pulled out at the bottom and the bedspread was on the floor.

Lark walked over and stood looking down at the girl's ravaged face. Every inch of visible skin was covered with angry pustules, her eyes were red, and her hair was matted. She focused on Lark and licked her cracked lips. "Wh-what are you doing here?" she asked in a hoarse whisper.

Lark blinked back the tears that sprang to her eyes. She sat down on the side of the bed and took Candace's hot, pox-covered hand. "I just heard that you were ill. I've come to help take care of you if you'll let me."

Candace's glance sought her father, who stood next to Lark. "It's up to you, baby," Jonathan said, with no indication that he had a preference one way or the other.

Candace hesitated, then nodded. "Daddy needs some rest," she said, and looked away as she pulled her hand from Lark's.

Lark ignored the rebuff. "I'm going to look in on Patty now," she said as she stood. "Then I'll be back to see about making you more comfortable."

Back out in the hall Lark looked at Jonathan. "Candace is right," she said softly. "You do need rest. Why don't you—"

"Get one thing straight, Lark," he snapped. "You're here to help take care of the girls. I'm not part of the bargain, so do me a favor and leave me alone." He walked quickly away from her toward Patty's room.

Lark stung from the lash of his rebuke as she followed behind him.

Patty lay sleeping on the twin-size bed Jonathan had bought earlier, at Lark's request, to replace the crib. She had her two fingers in her mouth, and her tender baby skin was disfigured with the itchy pustules. Lark looked down at her and brushed a strand of fine wheat-colored hair away from her sensitive cheek. "Poor baby," she murmured, then spoke to Jonathan. "She doesn't feel as warm as Candace did."

"No," he answered, "her temperature started down as soon as she broke out. According to the doctor that's the normal course of the disease, but Candace has been broken out since early yesterday and her temp is still running between one hundred and three and one hundred and four degrees."

He motioned Lark to precede him out of the nursery. In the hall Lark said, "Is she getting medication?"

"Tylenol every few hours and sponge baths, plus some calamine lotion for the itching. Oh, and don't give either of them aspirin. The doctor was emphatic about that. There's evidence that aspirin given during chicken pox can cause Rey's syndrome later."

When they reached Candace's room they found her sitting on the edge of the bed. Lark hurried over to her. "Candace, you shouldn't try to get up. Can I get you something?"

"I'm going to the bathroom," Candace said, and stood up.

Lark put her arm around the girl's waist to steady her. "I'll go with you. If you feel up to it, maybe you'd like to take a quick shower."

Jonathan stepped back out of the way as Lark led Candace out of the room and down the hall to the bathroom. He was still there a few minutes later when she came back for a clean nightshirt and robe. "Jonathan, would you mind opening the blinds and the windows, and stripping the bed? I'll make it up with clean sheets as soon as I get Candace out of the shower."

He said nothing, but moved to open the blinds as she hurried back to the bathroom.

Lark adjusted the water to a comfortable temperature, then helped Candace undress and step under the shower. After the girl had washed and shampooed her hair, Lark dried her off with a soft towel and slipped the knee-length nightshirt over her head before wrapping her in a warm robe to ward off a chill. A smaller towel wrapped around her head turban-style helped to dry her long hair as Lark helped her back to her bedroom.

The room had been amazingly transformed. The blinds were pulled to the top, and the windows fully opened to let in the fresh breeze. The bed had been remade with clean pastel percale sheets, and the dirty linen, clothes and dishes had disappeared. Lark settled her patient in the bed, then adjusted the windows and blinds so that it would be light and airy, but not glaring or chilly. By the time she left to check on Patty, Candace was sleeping peacefully.

Lark repeated the procedure with Patty, and since her temperature was only slightly elevated, she took her downstairs to lie on the couch while Jonathan cleaned the house and Lark fixed rich homemade vegetable soup and a nourishing chicken and broccoli casserole.

That evening both the girls managed to eat all the soup in their bowls, although Candace still complained about the constant stream of liquids Lark insisted she drink. "I'll float, for heaven's sake," she wailed, but she continued to sip while Lark plumped up her pillows and covered her itching skin with a layer of calamine lotion in an effort to make her comfortable for the night.

Patty also got her covering of the chalky lotion before Jonathan came in to tuck her into bed.

The doorbell rang as Lark was on her way downstairs to clean up after dinner. She answered it and found Rob standing on the porch holding her several packed suitcases. He greeted her with a questioning look as she stepped back and motioned him to set the luggage on the floor in the entryway. "Melanie said you needed these," he said. "I assume that means you'll be staying here for a while?"

Lark shut the door but didn't invite him any farther into the house. "No need to play the big-brother role," she said amiably. "Jonathan was desperate for help, but that's all he's willing to accept from me. I won't be here more than a couple of days, three at the most."

Rob looked around. "How are the kids?"

"Patty's coming along nicely, but Candace is still pretty sick. She seems content to have me here, though."

"Have you told him about finding Giselle?"

Lark put her finger to her lips in a shushing motion. "He's upstairs reading a bedtime story to Patty," she explained. "No, I've been so busy since I got here that I haven't had a chance to tell him yet. I will when he comes down, so why don't you run along before he catches sight of you and throws us both out."

Rob opened the door and turned to leave. "Call me if you need me, hear?"

Lark nodded, then watched until he got into his car and drove away.

She'd just shut the door when Jonathan came downstairs. "Who was that?" he asked.

"It was Rob. He brought my clothes." She nodded toward the suitcases on the floor, then gave a short, bitter laugh at his look of consternation. "I'm not moving in," she said. "I was packing to leave for Phoenix tomorrow when I heard about Candace and Patty, so when I talked to Melanie I told her to just finish the packing and send everything over here rather than try to sort out the clothes I'd need for a short stay."

"You're going back to Phoenix?"

"Yes. As soon as the girls are well enough that I'm not needed here any longer. I would have left sooner but—" She cut short the explanation she should never have started.

Jonathan wasn't going to let her get away with it. "But what?" he insisted.

"Nothing. I—I just didn't feel up to driving so far earlier."

His glance traveled over her face and body. "You don't look like you're up to the drive now, either. You've got dark circles under your eyes, and you've lost weight. What's the matter? Have you been sick, too?"

She averted her eyes. "No, I'm fine." She stooped to pick up one of the cases. "Is it all right if I sleep upstairs in one of the spare rooms? I'll be able to hear the girls better from there if they need me in the night."

For a moment his gaze continued to search her face, then he picked up the rest of the luggage and turned toward the stairs. "Suit yourself," he said.

When Lark had finished settling into her room, she went back downstairs to clean up the kitchen. Jonathan was nowhere in evidence, and she wondered if he'd gone to bed. She hoped so; he was exhausted from days of tending his sick daughters with very little rest. He needed a full night of unbroken sleep or he was going to be sick too.

As she stacked the dishes in the dishwasher she wondered what kind of patient he'd be, and a smile played at the corners of her mouth. Impossible, that's what kind. If he needed care, she'd have to fight him every inch of the way to give it to him. Why did he have to be so stubborn? Couldn't he tell how much she loved him? How sorry she was for deceiving him? Had he really managed to turn off his feelings for her as completely as he wanted her to believe?

It was almost eleven o'clock by the time Lark finished in the kitchen, and she was tired. She hadn't sat down except to eat all day, and she expected to have her sleep interrupted several times during the night. It was time to go to bed.

She still hadn't heard Jonathan stirring around, and a quick search of the main floor revealed that he wasn't there. He must be in his room.

She took a long hot shower in the downstairs bathroom so as not to disturb anyone upstairs, then slipped on her lilac chiffon nightie and brushed her hair. She'd forgotten to bring down her robe and slippers, but it didn't matter. Everyone else in the house was sleeping.

She gathered up her things and carried them up to her room, then left again to check on Candace and Patty. Candace was awake and fretful. Lark took her temperature, then gave her more Tylenol and water and touched up her itchy spots with calamine lotion.

Patty was asleep, curled up with a soft teddy bear. Her forehead was damp from sleep but not feverish, and her breathing was normal. Lark adjusted the blanket over her and was starting to leave when, in the dim light of the night lamp, she saw the door that connected the nursery and the master bedroom. She knew it was never locked, and she was still vaguely uneasy about Jonathan. She hadn't seen or heard him since he'd deposited her luggage in her room and disappeared.

Lark edged toward the door. He must be in there; she knew he hadn't left the house. Surely it wouldn't hurt if she just opened the door and looked in to make sure he was all right. She'd been startled at how badly he'd looked when she first saw him, and he hadn't rested at all during the day.

Without waiting to debate the pros and cons of it, she turned the knob and pushed open the door. The room was dark, but in the moonlight coming through the French doors that led to the redwood deck she could see a figure in the bed. She stood there, knowing she should back out but unable to bring herself to do so.

Slowly her bare feet inched across the carpet until she was standing beside the king-size bed. Jonathan was lying on his side, clad in pajamas but with the bedding thrown back. His breathing was regular and he seemed to be sleeping peacefully.

Now that she knew he was all right it was time for her to get out of there, go back to her own room. She stood looking down at him, telling her feet to move, but they seemed firmly rooted to the floor. While she was here, would it be so wrong of her to touch him? He was asleep and would never know, and when he was awake he wouldn't let her near. Surely just one light kiss on the cheek...

She bent over, careful not to bump the bed, and gently kissed him just above the line of his short beard. He smelled of soap. She moved her head an inch or so and brushed her lips across his closed eyelid, but before she could straighten up, two arms clamped around her, tumbling her onto the bed beside him.

A cry of surprise escaped her, but she quieted as he pulled her against him. "Damn you, Lark," he growled. "Why did you come in here? I told you to leave me alone."

She fitted herself against the long length of him. "I was worried about you," she said, and her voice was breathless. "You didn't say good-night, and you looked so worn out."

His arms tightened around her. "Why shouldn't I be? I haven't slept worth a damn since you left."

"Neither have I," she said, and worked her hand under his pajama coat to rub his bare back.

His muscles twitched under her palm, but he began to relax. "Is that why you didn't feel well enough to drive to Arizona?"

"Partly," she admitted. "I couldn't eat, either, and I couldn't seem to stop crying."

"Sounds like the flu," he said skeptically.

"No, my darling, no flu," she said softly. "It's unrequited love, and it's a hundred times worse than the flu."

"Tell me about it," he said sarcastically, then put his fingers to her mouth. "No, don't talk. I don't want to hear any more of your lies. I just want to hold you, feel you snuggled against me, until I fall asleep. I don't want to need you, Lark, but tonight I do. Just please, don't leave me until I get to sleep."

She continued to massage his back with her hand. If only she could tell him that she'd never leave him again if he'd only ask her to stay, but she knew he didn't want to hear that.

Lark was just starting to doze when she remembered that she still hadn't told Jonathan that Rob had found Giselle. He lay totally relaxed beside her except for the strength of his arms holding her. She knew he was asleep, but she had to wake him. If she didn't tell him now, he'd accuse her of withholding information for some sinister purpose when she finally did.

She twisted in his embrace, trying to rouse him, but his arms tightened and although his speech was slurred she distinctly heard him say, "Don't leave me, Lark. Oh, God, how I love you."

She cuddled against him and sobbed into his shoulder. She wasn't sure if they were tears of joy or despair. She knew he was speaking the truth—he was too far asleep not to— but she was sure he'd never admit it when he was awake.

He thought that loving her was a weakness he had to overcome.

Jonathan awoke slowly the next morning feeling rested and alert. Unlike the last time he'd slept that soundly, he knew what was missing from his bed. Lark. There was no sign of her ever having been there.

Well, what had he expected? He'd as much as told her to go back to her own room as soon as he got to sleep.

He'd done the right thing, but how long would it be before the pain stopped tearing his insides apart? Not for the first time he wondered why men were denied the release women found in tears. How come it was more manly to develop ulcers?

He glanced at the bedside clock, then checked it with his watch. Good heavens, it was nearly noon. He'd slept almost twelve hours. A shiver ran through him as he remembered how she'd felt cuddled in his embrace with nothing on but that flimsy nightgown.

He got out of bed and dressed in jeans and a sweatshirt, then looked at his clock again. The last time he'd slept this long was the time he'd slept with Lark. How come the one woman who kept him in an almost constant state of arousal was also the one who could lull him to such a sound sleep when he got her in bed?

"Nolan," he told himself bitterly. "You're coming unglued."

Lark ladled fragrant chicken noodle soup into a bowl and placed it and a glass of cranberry juice on a bed tray for Candace. She had just glanced across the room at Patty, who was sitting in her high chair drinking soup out of a mug, when Jonathan came into the kitchen.

"Good morning," he said brightly, and Lark was relieved to see that he looked rested. "Or is it afternoon?" he added, and walked over to kiss Patty on top of her tousled head. "Hi, baby. You feel cooler this morning."

He had only glanced at Lark, but she assumed he expected a response to that last statement. "Her temperature's normal, and she's feeling better," she said. "That's her second cup of soup."

He looked up and smiled. "That's good to hear." He sniffed. "Mmm, something smells good."

Lark smiled back. "My mother's recipe for homemade chicken noodle soup, except that I don't make the noodles, I use the packaged kind."

"Do you suppose you could spare some of it for the starving master of the house?" he teased, and Lark was delighted with his light mood.

"If you can wait just a few minutes until I take this tray to Candace," she said, and picked it up.

Jonathan came to her side and took it from her. "I'll do it," he said. "I stopped in her room on the way down, and she's looking better too."

"Her temperature's down to a hundred and one. It's still high, but I think it's finally broken."

"Thank God," he said fervently, and walked out of the room.

Lark was puzzled. He was in a better humor today, but so far he hadn't said a word about pulling her into bed with him last night. Had he forgotten? It was possible. He'd only been awake for a few minutes, and he'd slept soundly both before and after the episode.

Patty had cried out at one o'clock, but he hadn't moved at all when Lark crawled out of his arms and went to her. After Patty had settled down again, Lark had gone back to her own room, and a couple of hours later Candace needed attention. Then at six-thirty Patty was wide awake and insisted on getting up, so Lark hadn't had much sleep, but Jonathan had virtually collapsed and heard nothing.

Yes, it was very probable that he had no memory of taking her into his bed, and she was sure he didn't remember telling her that he loved her.

While Jonathan was upstairs with Candace, Lark put Patty back to bed for a nap.

Lark had the soup and tuna fish sandwiches ready when he came back, and after she'd poured the coffee she picked up the thick file folder lying on the counter and joined him at the table. This was something that couldn't wait another minute.

"Jonathan," she said hesitantly, hating to interrupt his meal. "I called your office yesterday morning to make an appointment to see you. That's how I found out the girls were ill."

He stopped eating and looked at her. "Oh?"

She cleared her throat. "Yes. I—we had some news for you, and Rob thought I should be the one to tell you."

Jonathan said nothing but continued to watch her as he waited for her to continue.

She lifted her chin and squared her shoulders. "Rob's found Giselle. She's married to a man named Juan Alvarez and works at one of the gambling casinos in Las Vegas."

Jonathan put down his spoon. "I see," he said, and his good mood was gone. "So why did you wait twenty-four hours to tell me?"

She'd been afraid he'd take that attitude. "When your secretary told me your daughters were ill, I forgot everything else. I didn't think of it again until Rob asked about it when he brought my clothes over. I meant to tell you then, but you went right to bed and I didn't see you again. I'm sorry. I didn't deliberately keep it from you."

He frowned, but he didn't pursue the criticism. "How long has she been married, and why didn't she get in touch with any of us?"

Lark picked up the file folder and handed it to him. "I don't know any of the details, but Rob brought this copy of the report for you. I assume they're all in here."

Jonathan took the folder and laid it on the table beside him. "You should give this to the Ulrics," he said bitterly. "They're the ones you worked for."

She sighed. She should have known better than to hope he might forgive her. "They'll get one too, of course, but Rob completed the search for Giselle on his own. He hasn't worked for them since the day you threw us all out of the house. They called off the investigation."

"Then why did your brother continue with it?" He didn't sound pleased. She had thought that the relief of knowing Giselle was safe and happy might cancel out some of the bitterness, but obviously it hadn't.

She shrugged. "I didn't know until yesterday that he had, but I suppose he didn't like leaving a case unfinished. Maybe he did it for me."

"Your curiosity wouldn't be satisfied until you knew the whole story, is that it?" He pushed away from the table and stood. "Well, now you can go back to Phoenix with a clear conscience. All the loose ends have been tied up nice and neat."

He stalked out of the kitchen without finishing his lunch.

The rest of the day was all downhill. She saw little of Jonathan, and when she did he was cool and silent, speaking to her only when necessary. Lark knew it was time to think of leaving.

By evening Patty's temperature had been normal all day and she was happily playing around the house, itchy but otherwise none the worse for her illness. Candace's temp had been dropping, and it now hovered around a hundred degrees. She was more alert, and the headache that had plagued her was gone. Jonathan had told her that her mother had been found, but she didn't talk about it to Lark.

While Lark was making her comfortable for the night, Candace reached out and hugged her. "Thanks, Lark," she said shyly, "you've made me feel so much better since you've been here. I've missed you. I'm glad you came back."

Lark battled the ever ready tears as she returned the hug. She couldn't bring herself to tell the girl that she'd be leaving again very soon.

Lark slept soundly that night, and when she woke at nine o'clock the next morning Jonathan was gone and Patty was watching Saturday morning cartoons on television in Candace's room. In the kitchen she found a terse note from Jonathan, telling her he'd gone to the office to catch up on the work he'd neglected the past week, but that he'd be home in time for dinner.

By early afternoon Candace's temperature had returned to normal, and she felt well enough to put on her robe and go downstairs to lie on the couch. By Monday, when Jonathan would have to return to work, she would be well enough to be left alone with Patty during the day.

It was time for Lark to leave. Each day she stayed made it more painful to go, and she couldn't stand much more anguish.

Later in the day, while Patty napped and the thick stew she was preparing for dinner simmered in the heavy Dutch oven, Lark took a long leisurely bath and dressed in a moss green silk dress, sleeveless, with a draped neckline and a dropped waist encircled with a hipband. It was too dressy for dinner at home with the children, but it would be her last evening with the Nolan family and she needed the boost it gave her. Then she repacked her bags and had the meal ready to serve when Jonathan arrived.

If she'd hoped to impress him she needn't have bothered. His shuttered look when he saw her told her nothing, but he was relieved to find his daughters so much better. Candace ate at the table with them for the first time, and she chatted happily, unaware of her father's thoughtful silence.

Lark was more finely tuned to Jonathan's moods, and she assumed he was trying to find a diplomatic way to tell her that her services were no longer needed. She decided to make it easy for him, and at the next lull she said, "I'm so happy that you're well enough to be up and around, Candace. Especially since I really can't postpone my trip home any longer."

Jonathan's fork clattered on his plate, and Candace looked at her uncomprehendingly. "Home?" she said. "But you are home, Lark."

Lark made a valiant effort to smile. "No, honey, I mean my home in Phoenix. I never intended to be gone so long. I'll spend tonight with Rob and Melanie, then leave early tomorrow for Arizona."

"You're going to *Phoenix*?" Candace's brown eyes were round with disbelief. "But you came back to us. I don't want you to go." She sounded as unbelieving as she looked.

Just then Patty, aware that something was wrong but not sure what, began to wail. Without a word, Jonathan picked her up and carried her out of the room, leaving Lark to explain to Candace.

Lark took Candace's hand in hers. "Candace, you were there the day your father found out I'd deceived him. He was furious, and with good cause. He hasn't forgiven me; he just let me take care of you and Patty these last few days because he was desperate for help. He won't even listen to me when I try to tell him how much I love him, how much I love you and Patty. I never meant to hurt any of you, but I did and now he doesn't trust me."

"I'll talk to him," Candace said eagerly. "I'll make him listen."

"No!" Lark clutched the hand she held. "No, Candace, you mustn't interfere. I couldn't stand it if I thought I'd come between you and Jonathan. Just leave it alone, honey. You can't force one person to love another. Love has to come naturally or not at all."

After a few tears and promises to write often, Candace was persuaded to go to bed. Lark went up with her to kiss Patty good night. She didn't explain to the little one that she was leaving. There was no need to upset her, Lark told herself. She'd accept it better if Lark was just gone the next morning.

Lark stopped in the bathroom to splash cold water on her face and try to undo some of the damage her anguish had caused. She looked awful. Her eyes seemed swollen to twice their normal size, and they were dark with the pain she couldn't disguise. Why did loving have to hurt so?

When she got back downstairs she found Jonathan in the kitchen stacking dirty dishes in the dishwasher. He looked up when she came in, and for a moment she saw the tormented indecision in his eyes. What was he indecisive about? Oh, well, it didn't matter anymore.

"I was going to do that, Jonathan," she said, carefully controlling her voice, which had an unfortunate tendency to quiver.

He continued what he was doing. "I'm almost finished. Go into the den and wait for me, Lark. I want to talk to you."

A sense of panic pervaded her. She couldn't talk to him. She had to get out of there before she broke down. "I—I don't think we have anything more to say. I'll just go up and get my luggage." She turned and fled.

Upstairs in her room she looked around to make sure she'd gotten everything, then slung the long strap of her purse over her shoulder and picked up her two largest suitcases. She'd have to come back up again for the overnighter and cosmetic kit.

She turned and took a step forward before she saw Jonathan blocking the doorway. She stopped as he silently shut and locked the door, then walked over to her and took the bags out of her hands and set them on the floor. "I can't let you go again, Lark," he said, but he sounded sad.

She felt a stab of hope, but it was dashed by his grim countenance. "You don't sound very happy about it," she pointed out.

"I'm not," he answered, still not touching her. "I was tricked into marriage once, and I swore I'd never let that happen again. I hadn't counted on falling in love."

Her heart pounded. This is what she'd prayed would happen, but it wasn't going the way she'd imagined it at all. Her good sense told her to probe further, even as her heart told her to accept whatever he had to offer. "Are you saying I tricked you into falling in love?" she asked anxiously.

He reached out then and pulled her into his embrace, and she realized he was trembling. He was as unsure and upset as she was. She relaxed against him and put her arms around his neck, where they'd ached for so long to be. "Oh my darling," she murmured, "why won't you believe that I love you? Haven't I shown you in every way that I could?"

"I want to believe it," he said unsteadily. "I'd sell my soul to believe it, but you tricked me into hiring you; you went behind my back to get information I wouldn't have given you voluntarily; you deliberately set out to deceive me."

She ran her fingers through the dark hair at the back of his head. "I've already admitted all that. I've told you I was wrong, said I was sorry; but I was always honest about my feelings for you. When you kissed me, held me, made love to me, I responded because I wanted you as much as you wanted me."

As she spoke his hands roamed over her back, and he trailed tiny kisses down the side of her neck, causing her to lose track of what she was saying. "Jonathan," she scolded happily, "you're not paying attention."

"Yes I am," he said, and nibbled on her earlobe. "You said you wanted me." His wandering hand found her breast and settled there.

She made a massive effort to gather her scattered thoughts. "Actually, I was more honest about my feelings than you were. I knew I was in love with you, but you kept telling me you'd never fall in love again."

"I lied," he muttered as he found the zipper at the back of her dress and pulled it down. "Or rather, I wouldn't admit even to myself the depth of my feelings for you. I knew I'd just be hurt again."

His arms found the bare flesh of her waist under her dress, and he raised his head until his mouth found hers in a soul-stirring kiss that left her shivering with need. While his tongue alternately plundered and caressed, Lark lowered her arms and let the purse and her dress drop to the floor. Jonathan unhooked her bra and slipped it off her shoulders, sending it to join the dress.

He moved them the few steps to the side of the bed, then reached down and threw back the covers, but when she started to unbutton his shirt he put his hand over hers to stop her. "Before this goes any further," he said in a voice hoarse with strain, "there's one thing I have to know. Lark, my sweet, warm and generous love, will you marry me?"

She'd wanted so badly to hear those words, but they didn't hold the promise she'd expected. Her fingers continued with the buttons despite his light restraint. "Why have you changed your mind, Jonathan?" she asked. "You told me that you'd never marry again, and I'm sure you meant it. I give you my love freely; there are no conditions. I'll make love with you whether you marry me or not."

For a moment he was silent, then he lifted her face and gazed deeply into her troubled green eyes. "What would happen if I kept you around for a few months and then sent you away?"

She blinked, hoping he wouldn't read the agony in her eyes. "I'd shatter into a million splinters," she said, "but it would be no different than if we were married and you asked for a divorce. I'm afraid I'm committed to you for life, but I'm not demanding the same commitment from you. I don't want you to make vows you can't keep."

With a muttered curse he wrapped her in his embrace, and she felt the sob that shook him before he could get it under control. "Vows I can't keep," he repeated in a voice that trembled. "Oh my precious darling, whether we take vows or not, once you've given yourself to me in the intimacy of love, I'll never let you go. My former marriage was a sham, but with you it'll be for life. I need you now and forever. Are you willing to spend the rest of your life with me?"

Lark felt as if she had come out of fog into the sunshine and her smile was tremulous as she brushed his lips with her own. "I'll marry you first thing in the morning if that's what you want," she said happily, "but right now I'd really like to get on with what we've started. Now, are you going to remove that shirt, or do I have to tear it off you?"

He took quick possession of her elusive lips, and stoked the fire that had been building between them. "Sweetheart," he murmured when they came up for air, "you can tear my clothes off me anytime."

COMING NEXT MONTH

RELUCTANT DREAMER—Dixie Browning
Her son and her gift shop were Portia's whole life, until Cole Randolph showed up. They clashed at every turn, but neither wanted to deny the love growing between them.

YESTERDAY ONCE MORE—Debbie Macomber
The most difficult decision Julie had ever made was to leave Kansas. But her heart demanded that she return and fight for Daniel's love.

LADY OF THE WEST—Jennifer Mikels
Her authentic frontier town was in trouble, so Tory advertised for help. Enter stage left: actor Josh Bannion, former cinema sex symbol. Enter stage right: love.

LOVE BUG—Kat Adams
After slaughtering Kelley's snapdragons, thirteen-year-old J. T. Landers came up with the perfect idea: fix Kelley up with his widowed father, Jason. His willing partner in crime—Kelley's daughter, Leigh.

JUST ONE LOOK—Jude O'Neill
Their relationship was a fast-paced thirties comedy film. Could Zan and Stu's love survive icy dunkings in San Francisco Bay and three cheerfully interfering old women? Sure—after a muddy, slippery bicycle ride.

LAS VEGAS MATCH—Barbara Turner
Jenna was determined to save her sister from that ruthless man, so she tricked Kirby Carmichael into "marrying" her. What she didn't know was that their "phony" marriage was real—and that Kirby had no intention of telling her.

AVAILABLE THIS MONTH:

GALLAGHER'S LADY
Brittany Young

MAN BY THE FIRE
Victoria Glenn

AN HONEST LOVER
Phyllis Halldorson

THE ROMANTIC AND THE REALIST
Barbara Bartholomew

MYSTERIES OF THE HEART
Ruth Langan

LOVE IS FOREVER
Tracy Sinclair

**Available
October 1986**

California Copper

The second in an exciting new
Desire Trilogy by Joan Hohl.

If you fell in love with Thackery—the
laconic charmer of *Texas Gold*—you're
sure to feel the same about his twin
brother, Zackery.

In *California Copper*, Zackery meets the
beautiful Aubrey Mason on the windswept
Pacific coast. Tormented by memories,
Aubrey has only to trust...to embrace
Zack's flame...and he can ignite the fire in
her heart.

The trilogy continues when you
meet Kit Aimsley, the twins' half
sister, in *Nevada Silver*. Look for
Nevada Silver—coming soon from
Silhouette Books.

Silhouette Special Edition

Sophisticated and moving, these expanded romances delight and capture your imagination book after book. A rich mix of complex plots, realism and adventure.